The Lines We Draw

(Artists and Athletes book 1)

By CD Rachels

The Lines We Draw

Cover Illustration Copyright © Story Styling Cover Designs
Professional beta read by Catherine at Les Court Services. https:// www.lescourtauthorservices.com

(Synopsis)

Ravi

I'm perfectly fine in my comfort zone. As co-captain of my university soccer team, I know my place. I play hard on the field and my teammates look up to me. Would they look up to me if they knew I liked guys? Probably not, so I'm okay staying a closeted virgin.

That is, until I'm forced to take an arts class, and I'm seated next to the sexiest guy I've ever seen. He helps me pass art class, makes me laugh, and has me wanting things I never thought were possible. As the semester goes on, we get closer, and trying to keep my hands off him and stay away from him becomes nearly impossible.

What will happen to my position on the team if I ask him out? I don't think I'm willing to find out. Now I just gotta stop dreaming about kissing him and holding him... Damn.

Steven

* * *

As a fine arts major, I have to focus on creating good work and impressing my professors. Part of that entails sitting in on this beginners arts class, and I just so happen to be next to a gorgeous athlete this semester.

Relationships are a sour note for me, but flirting with the co-captain of the soccer team could be fun. I know it's not going to go anywhere- he's straight. Over time, though, becoming friends with Ravi, teaching him how to visualize his art, and learning about his life makes me question what we're doing.

I don't know if I'm ready to let someone else into my heart again, least of all a potential closet case (no matter how sexy he is). Still, with the way he makes me smile and how my heart beats when I'm near him, I think we're both in too deep now.

["The Lines We Draw" is a low-angst, friends-to-lovers story involving art classes, soccer games, nude models, drunken parties, and discovering what sex and love can really feel like, HEA guaranteed.

It is the first of a series and can be read as a standalone.]

To J. Thanks for playing video games while I did this.
To Rachel and Rod. For being my number one fans.

1: Ravi

I've always felt fairly confident during my time here at Korham University. Things didn't really shake me because I understood my place here on campus: I'm a junior year business major, but first and foremost, I'm a soccer player. As co-captain of our Division 2 soccer team, I know what I'm supposed to do, day in and day out.

I go to practice, hang out with my teammates, then go back to the designated athletes' dorm, which, naturally, is filled with my teammates as well. I go to classes, listen to my coaches, and on the field, I work hard. I'm known on the team as the "quiet leader", but that's just because I don't come off as the "party boy" stereotype like some of my more socially-inclined companions. I'm not loud, I don't obnoxiously regale my teammates about dumb stories about my sex life, and even at parties, I avoid getting messy.

Quietness is my comfort zone, and my comfort zone is where I'd like to stay. Unfortunately, I go to a liberal arts university, which is structured around "pushing boundaries" as the pamphlets like to say. I call it more of "pissing me off" because, frankly, I don't see the appeal of having to take an arts class. Nevertheless, this university offered me a massive scholarship and had a lot of cool athletic facilities when I visited, so here I am. According to my advisor, I need one of these classes to fulfill my undergraduate requirements. If I don't pass this class, it will completely mess up my practice schedule for next year, or worse- I won't get to graduate on time. The stakes are kind of high, which is why today, I find myself entering the fine arts building.

In my over two years here, I had yet to walk through the red-brick-lined three story building on the other side of campus, far from the soccer field, but not too far from my dorm. I knew it existed, but I thought it was only for people who did ballet or played the harp or something. I legitimately thought I would never have to step foot in the building, yet here I am, passing another set of double doors and walking up a staircase trying to find room 311.

All of this is to take a class that puts me so far out of my comfort zone that my comfort zone is effectively a dot. A black dot... Or a black line... Making a dark black stick figure line man- which is exactly what my artistic prowess can create. I can only hope I make it through this semester taking "Drawing and Inking 101". The fact of the matter is: DI101 was the only low-level liberal arts course that fit in with my practice schedule that seemed to promise to NOT humiliate me as much as possible. I can't play an instrument, I refuse to wear a leotard, but I CAN, however, hold a pencil. I think. I hope.

I can see the school newspaper headline now: *"Ravi Metta:*

Artist in Residence and his Stick Figure Portraits."

As I walk through the metal door labeled "311," I slowly survey the room. There are several large wooden tables with metal stools lining them, and they are filling up fast (about 4 for each of the four tables). Large windows overlook the inner courtyard of the fine arts building, but at an angle so that the people down there can't see much in here. The professor, an older stout woman with flowing gray curls, is handing out what I assume is the syllabus, so I immediately dash to take an available stool. It's far enough that there's one person across from me, looking at the professor. I sit between the table and a window sill, as far away from everyone as possible. Here I find solitude, my old familiar friend, in a course that's giving me anxiety already, but I'm not sure why.

Who am I kidding? Someone like me is always anxious. I'm quiet and keep to myself and play my part on the soccer team because the truth is I want to keep my personal life private. I don't want people to know that I don't want to date all the girls my friends talk about or try to set me up with. I fantasize at night about someone with stubble, a deep voice, and a musky, testostcrone-filled scent. I recall back in ninth grade summer camp, holding hands with a boy during a movie night, but being too chicken-shit to do anything else with a guy then. That's what the "comfort zone" really is: a clubhouse for people who are too afraid to want anything else or do anything about it. I dream about a guy who can see me as more than some dumb, closeted jock who's afraid of his own identity.

Of course, the moment I think that, he decides to enter the room; a guy about my height with fair skin walks through the double doors with a confident step and an easy smile.

3

He's wearing a grey beanie hat, skin-tight blue jeans, and a blue backpack slung over one shoulder. He nods and smiles to a bunch of the other artsy kids in the class, as well as the professor. He sits down next to me and I have to fight the urge to rotate my stool and stare at him.

See, it's not just that he's naturally handsome (he is). It's not just that he's sitting so close to me that I can smell him and he smells great (that's also true). It's also not the eyebrow piercing and perfect hazel eyes or confident smile and... fuck, is that stubble? No it's not any of that; it's because he's wearing a rainbow bracelet among various other accessories. That means the likelihood of him being gay went from 99 to a whopping 100%. This guy, this handsome, sexy guy who is sitting WAY too close to me is everything I'm not. He's out and proud of his sexuality and he's owning his presence in the room. I stare down at the table (the nice, nice wooden table) in order to not drool over some random dude in my vicinity.

"Hey."

I look up to see those gorgeous eyes staring right at me.

"Could you umm..." Yes, whatever it is, I'll do it for you. Fuck, I've got it bad already, don't I? "Could you pass the syllabus?"

He points to my right. I see that I'm literally the only thing between him and a stack of papers.

"Uh... yeah," I stammer, grabbing the pile and plopping it down next to him without even bothering to look up. He smiles and nods.

"I'm Steven by the way." He smiles at me.

"Mmm... Ravi" I mutter.

"Mr. O'Rourke," says the booming feminine voice in front

4

of us. I turn to see the professor with an unimpressed look on her face. "I'm going over the syllabus. It's the first day for most of these students. So please, zip it." She says, as she walks away. "And on the first page you'll see the supply list." She continues to vocalize loudly to everyone else.

"Don't be afraid of Professor Irons, or Deirdre as I like to call her," says Steven, as I turn back to him, still in shock by literally everything that's happening around me. "She totally loves me. I'm her favorite." He shrugs and closes his eyes, smiling. "This semester is gonna be cake for us."

He said 'us'; apparently this gorgeous guy wants to torture me by being friends now? This semester... is gonna be rough. I miss my comfort zone, so, so bad.

5

2: Steven

I swivel in my chair from side to side while Deirdre drones on and on. "Lastly this is where we keep the burnt plates and the oil for you to make your ink. Don't you DARE let me catch any of you putting paper, bags, or, heaven forbid, food or drinks in this area." She makes a leer at every one of the students except me.

I notice Ravi, the sexy, dark-skinned guy next to me looks terrified. It's kind of adorable. "Bro, don't sweat it. I'm here, and I won't steer you wrong." I smile at him, trying to ease his anxiety. He gives me a fake smile and goes back to looking slightly distraught.

"Now, for today, we have some charcoal and we're going to do some still-life's," says Prof. Irons. "Please proceed to take one of the scrap pieces of paper and charcoal from the two closets and begin setting up."

As everyone gets up, I see the guy next to me nervously looking down. "Hey man, I get it- you wanna get on her good

6

side on day one," I say, trying for a more pacifying tone. "Follow me. I'll show you where the good charcoal is." I tap him on his (very firm) shoulder with the back of my hand and get up as he follows me.

While everyone else rushes to the two closets, I walk straight for a far corner with the new guy in tow. "Here it is. The charcoal I left behind last semester. Premium shit." I smirk, picking up a box of large thick black cylinders.

"You... Uh, you took this class already?"

"Yeah man. Irons is letting me take my junior-year elective during her DI101 class time."

"Oh uh, cool," he replies, as if that was the worst possible answer.

I smile to try to cheer him up. "Yeah it's gonna be great, I'm really looking forward to creating new stuff: new ink combinations, even try some etching later on, it's gonna be sick." Ravi nods like I'm giving him a parking ticket while picking up a charcoal stylus.

"Alright well, we better get started on the still-life's or Deirdre will think I'm being a bad influence on you." I wink for good measure. Ravi seems taken aback by the gesture, but I regret nothing. Making hot guys like him blush is a rare occurrence that always makes my day better.

--

An hour-and-a-half later, all of us in class are packing up.

"Thanks um... for your help today," says Ravi.

"No problem. I'll see you in class on Wednesday!"

"Yeah sure. Um... I'm Ravi by the way."

"I know" I smile, "You told me when class started."

"Oh uh, duh, of course," he says, shaking his head and waving his hand in front of him.

"You got some charcoal on the side of your hand man, let me..." I trail off as I wipe at his hand with part of my shirt.

Ravi's eyes dart for anywhere except my eyes as he steps back and says, "Uh thanks. See ya." He proceeds to make a quick getaway. I smile as I push the black dust off my shirt.

"Making friends?" I look up to see my friend Simone walking over, bag of art supplies over her shoulder.

"I'm always friendly," I reply, matching her smirk. There aren't too many people around now, and no one's listening to us.

"Yeah, a little too friendly. That guy looked like he couldn't get out of here fast enough."

"Yeah well, I guess art isn't really his thing. I bet it's the KU liberal arts mandate and all that crap."

"He's pretty good-looking though," says Simone.

"I guess, in a 'Captain-of-the-Basketball' team sorta way."

"Soccer."

"What?"

"He's captain of the soccer team."

"Shut up!" I whisper, my eyes getting serious. "You're lying."

"For real," she replies, as we finally stroll out of the studio.

"Damn... and he's in OUR art class"

"Don't you know how to choose them," she remarks.

"What's THAT supposed to mean?" I ask, knowing damn well what she means.

"It means I know you've been single for awhile, but all of the soccer guys are straight, as far as I'm aware. Going after him seems like, I don't know, a waste of time?"

"It's not a waste of time, 'cause I'm not going after him. I'm just... being friendly."

"Uh huh. Sure" She smiles that toothy grin. "Come on, let's

go get dinner."

"Alright."

"Hey there's a dining hall by the jock dorm," she says, in a sing-song tone, holding my arm. "Let's go there and make some MORE new friends."

"Fuck you." I laugh as I drag her pointedly AWAY from the athlete's dorms.

Simone had a point though. After dating my exboyfriend Sean for the second half of high school and freshman year, relationships were kind of a sour note for me. If someone who liked all the same things as me and was openly gay and had so much in common with me (all of the things Sean was) could just decide that he wasn't in love with me anymore, it kind of messes a guy up. That's not even counting the closeted jock I was hooking up with before Sean- that was somehow even worse.

With my relationship disasters, I eventually just started to feel like I didn't deserve a real relationship, or I'm not worth loving. For now, flirting with guys who I know would never date me seems like the safer, more comfortable option.

Celibacy is easier for the time being (as horny as I may be). I need to focus on my fine arts degree and my end-of-semester exhibition. If getting friendly with a sexy soccer star is part of art class, then so be it. It's just a little flirting- what harm could it do?

3: Ravi

I fling my shirt off, soaked in sweat, as I walk into the locker room. It's our third practice of the semester, but our coach already has us running ragged, doing extra drills with minimal breaks. The team has big shoes to fill considering how well the graduating seniors played off of each other, so the pressure was on, for sure.

Despite my aching legs, the rough practice suited me just fine. The soccer field is my home turf; I'm at ease doing extra drills running back and forth. I find comfort in diverting all my thoughts on where to run to next, where to put the ball, and anticipating every other player's next move. All of it got my mind off of a certain art student who has decided to torture me with lust by becoming my friend Mondays and Wednesdays this semester.

Steven O'Rourke. As I shower, thoughts of him creep back into my mind (and I do NOT want to deal with a hard-on right now). I towel off and walk back to my locker while my friends and teammates follow suit, filling the locker room.

"Hey bro, so I'm thinking this weekend we could hit up downtown, maybe The Mousetrap?" My best friend Landon saddles up next to me while I quickly put on underwear and pants. He pushes his wet hair back while grinning at me in an effort to get me on board with his weekend plans.

Landon was what you might call a social butterfly, or a stereotypical jock, depending on your mood. He frequented parties, had a charming smile, and chased after girls constantly. We became fast friends at the athlete's summer orientation before school started freshman year, and we complimented each other well on and off the field. He made me have more of a social life, and I watered him down during his obnoxious prick-like moments.

"So you in?" he continues, as I finish putting on my clothes.

Realizing I hadn't replied in a beat, I say, "Uh yeah sure. Who else?" I nod to some of our other nearby friends.

"Kareem?"

"For sure, unless I have something going on," replies my tall, lean friend and co-captain, two lockers down.

"What do you mean 'Something going on'? There's no way you need to 'study.'" Landon uses air-quotes for that part and continues, "It's so early in the semester!"

"But coach said we need a C average to remain on the team," replies a freshman from across the room- Paul I think was his name? "Also, what's a Mousetrap?"

"THE Mousetrap," chimes in my other best friend, Omar, walking over from the other side of Paul. "...is a sick bar downtown. 'Sick' in the sense that it's a sweet vibe, but also 'sick' in the sense that we've all thrown up there at least once. It's truly magical." He wipes away fake tears of joy while the rest of us laugh.

"But I'm still a freshman. I'm only eighteen." Paul sounds

11

worried. The rest of the freshman are looking at us with interest but with a similar visage of concern.

"*I'm only eighteen,*" Landon whines in a mocking tone. "Well with THAT attitude I guess you can't come then froshie! No fun times for you!"

"Hey be nice," I interject, pointing at Landon and giving him a faux-stern look. I then turn to the freshman and add, "Your time to party will come eventually... uhh.. Paul?"

"Yes sir, uh captain." He says nervously.

"Please, it's Ravi." I smile.

"Oh no we are calling you SIR from now on, *mon capiTAN!*" laughs Omar with a salute, French accent, and everything.

"Yes sir!" laughs Landon, while Kareem salutes as well. Everyone has a laugh, and it feels like the heat is off Paul and the other freshmen. I can only hope they realize that we are no longer laughing at them (mostly).

"Look man, you do what you need to do. I barely hit the bars until I was 21," I reply to Paul. "Until then, study if you need to."

"Yeah, sure, later new guys!" says Landon as he pulls my shoulder to lead me out of the locker room.

The air is still warm as we walk to our building, despite the sun almost setting. The beginning of the semester still bites with summer heat, making our two-hour practices all the more brutal. Still, I loved soccer, I loved my spot on the team, and I even loved being captain to these knuckleheads I called my friends. Most importantly, I loved how comfortable I was on the field. I did what my coaches asked me and it all came naturally. The creative arts, talking to cute boys- these were all worries that plagued my mind, and I didn't want my friends to know that their captain was gay, or queer, or whatever label I'm supposed to be.

Out there, I'm team co-captain Ravi, and everything makes sense, but thinking about Steven... shit it had been a long time since I wanted to be so much more.

We pass by the dining hall convenience store to pick up some drinks and snacks, conveniently located outside the athletics dorm.

"It sucks that you're not free before practice anymore," says Landon while picking up a sports drink. "What are you taking again?"

"Drawing and Inking 101."

"Dude that sucks! Do you really need two hours per class to like, learn to draw something?"

"Actually yeah." I pick up some carrots and hummus. "There's all sorts of complicated ink and charcoal and materials; the class isn't a joke."

"Sorry. SO glad I don't have to take any arts classes at all."

"Bro, I'd check with your advisor, I'm almost positive everyone at KU needs to take an arts course."

"Not me. I'm a marketing-major-slash-soccer-star-slash-ladies-man. I'm untouchable." He grins and lifts his chin up, closing his eyes like the obnoxious bobble-head he is.

"OKAY Mr. Ladies-man." I roll my eyes and smile. "Let's go before we get trapped in here under the crushing weight of your expanding ego."

As he laughs and swipes his ID for his food, I dwell on all the dumbass comments he's made over the years. Would he and the rest of the team respect me knowing I don't wanna be a "ladies man" at all? If I wore a rainbow pride bracelet like Steven, would I still be welcome as team captain? Or in the locker rooms? These are the questions that keep me up at night.

4: Steven

CLAPCLAPCLAP.

"You know what that sound means!" Prof. Irons' voice howls over the rest of us. Her five-foot-something stature is accented by her hands raising a loud plastic trinket above. It's neon green and shaped like two hands, and as she waves it, the loud CLAPCLAPCLAP sound continues. "Class is over in 15 minutes. Clean up, then get out of my studio."

As most of the class proceeds to put away their work. I swivel to my right. "Be grateful she doesn't use a literal bell anymore. That shit was WAY worse."

I turn to Ravi to see him not moving, looking down in disappointment. His large paper is in front of him with this week's still-life mapped out in charcoal. "What's up man?"

"I'm really out of my... my everything here." He's still not looking up. His eyes might start blasting holes into the work soon if he keeps staring that way.

"What do you mean?"

"Professor Irons said to use a ruler to map out my drawing in grid format."

"Yeah?"

"The point was to like, I don't know... get a proper view or something."

"Yeah, assigning each square to be a sector of your view."

"Yeah, but mine still looks like crap after an hour," replies Ravi, dejectedly.

"Nah, man." I stand up and get his point of view by craning my neck closer to his shoulder. "Let me see." Up this close, I have to consciously ignore how good he smells. I thought he'd smell more like *"grass-stained soccer cleats"* not *"Abercrombie model,"* but I digress.

"It's... a work in progress."

"Nah. You're just being generous," says Ravi, still not looking up. "How am I going to start working on actual models or doing inking and etching next week? I need to do a decent job to pass this class, or I'll need to take another class that will just mess up my soccer schedule."

"That sounds rough."

"Word. If I can't do well here, I might actually lose my athletics scholarship."

An idea strikes me then. "Maybe I can help. I think I know exactly what you need." Upon saying this, Ravi finally turns to look up at me.

I'm mere inches away from his face, with my neck still almost touching his shoulder from behind. His eyes flare up at me in surprise, and I'm probably imagining him glancing at my lips for a brief second. "Wh-wh... what?" he stammers looking everywhere except me.

"You need a crash course on finding views and perspective, man. I take it you're not the kind of guy who just slows down to look at how landscapes actually exist, or, like, the puzzle pieces of natural scenery."

"The... the what?"

"Look," I chuckle. "You wanna get better right?" He nods. "Tomorrow. After dinner. You free?"

"I um, have practice until 6:30"

"Perfect. Meet me outside the clock tower after practice. I'll teach you one of my secrets to finding sight-lines that I've used for years." I smile and put a finger to my lip. "But you better not share- it's private. Deal?"

Ravi nods while putting his supplies away. If I didn't know he was on the soccer team (where all the guys are straight), I'd say he's blushing. He's adorable, which reminds me.

"Here, since we're working together so much," I hand over my phone with an open contact page. "Plug yourself in. So I can text you my droplets of fine arts wisdom as they flow through me throughout the day," I say, squinting and dramatically lifting my hand up with a faux-seriousness.

Ravi giggles as he plugs in his number. "You're a character, Steven. Here."

I take back my phone. "Well alright then. See you tomorrow for artistry boot camp."

His smile in that moment seems so genuine. As he looks into my eyes he seems so much more relaxed. "Can't wait."

Neither can I.

5: Ravi

After practice Friday, I take the long route around campus so that none of the guys follow me. I feel a little guilty lying earlier, saying that I need to talk to my art teacher; in a sense, it's a half-truth. I just didn't feel like dealing with the team ramblings if I told them, *"Hey, I'm hanging out with a guy from art class so he can teach me some techniques on how to see landscapes properly, and perhaps also flirt with him some more because I want to kiss his face- peace out!"*

Yeah sure, that would go over well. The guys on the team always talk about girls, and they call each other 'homo' as a joking insult. If they find out I'm actually gay, I'm sure those insults would just keep being hurled at me. I'm a captain, soccer is my place here at KU, and I need to command respect, even if that means staying the closet.

Yet, what am I doing hanging out with Steven outside of class? I think deep down, I want him to give me a reason to come out. I know for sure that I want him- his heart, his lips, and everything else.

As I approach the clock tower, I see a familiar figure in a grey beanie cap holding a blue backpack sitting on the bench.

"Hey," I say, out-of-breath, as I approach him. Why is my heart beating so fast?

"Hey yourself," grins Steven as he stands up. "Hope practice wasn't too bad."

"Nah it… it was fine." I stammer, running my fingers through my hair. He smiles at me, unconvinced.

"Alright well, follow me. I hope you're not too tired because we have some walking to do."

"Where to?"

"I told you Ravi, it's a secret." He once again puts his finger to his lips as he quickly strides past me.

--

We make our way past several parking lots on campus until we pass the property line of campus. We talk a little bit here-and-there about nothing in particular (which dorm I live in, what other classes I'm taking, etc.) as we walk. Now that we're not in class, I notice how surprisingly easy it is to talk to him.

We cross another street and turn right down a suburban sprawl of private houses. In my years here I had never seen any of this, so it seems to not be frequented by students, but was still only a ten-minute walk from the center of campus.

"Are you taking me somewhere to murder me? Some sort of fine arts prank or hazing?" I grin as we walk briskly on the sidewalk.

Steven chuckles. "I thought it was you jocks who did all the hazing."

"Hey, we're not all assholes," I retort, smiling. "I would never haze you."

"That's disappointing," he says, looking at me and

stopping. Why does it always feel like everything he says is a ploy to turn me on? Before I can question this, he says, "We're here" and points to his right.

I see a very small park tucked behind two houses; there's a playground, a concrete path, and a wooden bridge over a small stream, leading to a thicket of trees. The sky is a darkening blue as the sun is starting to set, but with the warmth in the air, it's a pretty perfect late summer evening.

"Wow, it looks nice," I muse as we make our way to the wooden bridge. "I've never heard of this place, how'd you find it?"

"Ehh." He shrugs. "I spend a lot of time walking alone. For all my yapping in art class, I actually do prefer peace and quiet."

"I feel that."

"It's weird, I know, but sometimes I need to get off campus and be away from everyone."

"Because you need to recharge. Be in a different environment. Judgment free, less noise." After saying this, I look up to find Steven staring at me, his expression one of surprise.

"Uh yeah... how'd you know that?"

"Stop stereotyping me, Steven," I say with a smirk. "Just 'cause I'm good at soccer doesn't mean I don't like long, quiet walks in nature."

That one earns a genuine smile. "Touché."

After a beat, he walks across the bridge and sits on a nearby tree stump. "Alright, so you've found my hiding spot. This is where I find my views." He proceeds to take out a sketchbook and pencil. As he begins to flip through it, he looks up at me. I'm looking directly at him, memorizing the way the setting sun catches his jawline through the trees. It's so quiet I swear I can hear my heart racing.

"Ravi, you're not gonna get any good views standing there looking at me!"

"*I beg to differ,*" I say to myself, smiling. Steven motions for me to join him and I sit next to him on the tree stump.

"Now look," he says, pointing upward toward a far off house. "What do you see?"

"Uhh… some houses? I don't know."

"Concentrate." He moves closer to me and once again puts his head near my shoulder. "Look where I'm looking." That's a tough order considering his thigh is touching mine, but I'm trying to not think about that. "See how the sunset is catching through that playground?"

"Yeah…"

"See what happens down there?" He points down with his right arm and his chest nearly touches my shoulder. I can barely breathe.

"There… on the ground?"

"It's…" he says, imploring me to continue.

"It's sight-lines?"

"Yes!"

"It's sight-lines!"

I honestly see it now. I can see how the light and shadow move and bend to compliment the landscape. I can see how the still-life's in class have those shadows as well. "I actually see it now!" I say louder, in delight.

"Congratulations." Steven's voice is a deeper tone than I'm used to. For what feels like the hundredth time this week, I turn my head to see him staring directly at me, inches from my face. My smile immediately fades. Fuck, he's right there. I could just…

"Here," he says, tearing a piece of paper with a loud rip. "Get to sketching, soccer captain." He smirks and hands me a pencil. I smile and nod and get to it. The beauty of the suburban sunset is what I'm supposed to be concentrating on right now, that's it. That's what my focus should be. I'm totally not going to be distracted by the gorgeous guy next to me. Nope, no way.

6: Steven

Twenty minutes have passed since Ravi and I sat down on this tree stump. Now, the street lights are on, and I'm starting to lose the ability to sketch in the darkness. I had sketched a fallen tree branch and later a squirrel that managed to stay put for a few seconds. It was moments like these that I really felt connected to everything: to Earth, to nature, and most importantly, to my craft. Sean always said it was weird that I enjoyed drawing the little things, like flowers, fallen apples, or acorns. He also didn't like that I needed to get away from it all sometimes. I think he always low-key resented my need for solitude.

In any case, I'm enjoying the quiet drawing time I have tonight. The entire time we're out here, Ravi is deep in concentration, and I don't have the heart to interrupt him. I occasionally look up, but he doesn't seem to notice, lost in whatever he's sketching. He looks so handsome with his eyebrows furrowed in concentration. Damn is he nice to look at.

"You almost finished buddy?" I finally ask, breaking him out of the spell.

"Yeah." Ravi makes some slight finishing touches, brushing away eraser dust. "I really see what you were talking about. This spot is perfect." He smiles fondly with pride.

I scoot over to look and he reflexively pulls back his paper. "Rude!" I say with feigned offense.

"Mine's not that..." he chuckles, clearly embarrassed.

"I wanna see what you got done!" I protest, I smiling.

"Uhh..." He looks down. "Only if I get to look through your sketchbook."

"Deal." I wanted to say, *"You show me yours, and I'll show you mine,"* but that would be too much- plus I don't want to ruin our moment.

I hand over my sketchbook while I take his paper. He's done some good work in the short time we've been here. His size ratios are consistent and he's even managed to do some legitimate shading, with some sides darker where they need to be. All in all, these drawings are an improvement from his work in class.

I'm about to compliment him when I look up and see he's gone way back into my sketchbook. I'm typically not embarrassed of my work, but there's something about Ravi that makes me only want to show him my best pieces. A lot of the stuff he's leafing through is stuff I did years ago and stuff I haven't showed anyone.

Despite this, even in the darkness, I can see him smiling. He seems to legitimately enjoy my work.

"Wow," he says. "This one is probably my favorite."

I get closer to see what he's referring to. It's a charcoal drawing of a mushroom on the side of a tree I did a year ago.

"That's just a mushroom."

"Yeah but you add so much detail. I get why you're the fine arts major. It's like you actually care. You see beauty in the smallest of subjects." My heart skips a beat in that moment and he's not even looking at me.

"Thanks," I reply softly. "Some people think my subjects arc... boring. Or lame."

"Well I don't think so," replies Ravi, smiling at me. I smile back as I slowly retrieve my sketchbook.

--

"Thanks for showing me all that stuff." Ravi and I are crossing the street back to campus. "Your hidden spot. And your work. You've got some really cool stuff." I feel the heat of a blush on my face.

"It... wasn't my best." I shrug.

"Well I liked it. You make pine cones and daffodils look epic with the amount of detail you put into them."

"Like I said, some people might say it's boring."

"Well you ought to surround yourself with cooler people." I can hear the smirk in his voice.

After a moment I stop underneath a streetlight. No one seems to be around. He pauses to look at me. "My exboyfriend Sean... he was the one who said it was lame." I awkwardly dig my shoe into the sidewalk. "He thought it was weird that I paid so much attention to the little things- the little things in nature, and in life. For a while I didn't show him or anyone those kinds of drawings."

"Well that's stupid," he retorts, his voice laced with concern. "His opinion. It was stupid of him to make you feel like your work wasn't... ya know... amazing. 'Cause it is." He smiles. "I'm glad you're not hiding it from me. Or anyone, anymore."

I return the smile and continue walking. "Me too."

We're approaching the dorms and dining halls when I hear Ravi speak again. "Steven, why DID you help me tonight?"

"Whadaya mean?"

"I feel like you're wasting time on the dumb, talentless jock." He's smirking at me.

"Maybe I like wasting my time on a dumb talentless jock," I tease.

"Ha ha." He rolls his eyes and raises his fist with a middle finger.

"Seriously," I reply, pushing down his middle finger. "What kind of fine arts major would I be if I didn't help a fellow art student in need? We're art buddies now." I grin.

My hand lingers on his fist. He seems to notice and looks directly down at it. I hear the sudden noise of a few people leaving the dining hall, and I awkwardly put my other hand over the rest of his fist. "Uhh.. peace out!" I say, with the worst rendition of a three-handed, pseudo-fist-bump-hand-shake.

I'm walking into the dining hall, not daring to look back at Ravi, when I see Simone and our other friend Jenny walk in as well. I hold the door open for both of them as I try to ignore Simone's suggestive smirk.

"Hey Steven," she says, her voice laced with suggestion. "Was that Ravi you were just with?"

"Yes," I reply curtly as we get into the cafeteria area.

"Is that the art class jock?" asks Jenny.

"Yes." I reply, gritting my teeth.

"Wow," says Simone. "You two certainly are..."

"Can we table this discussion until we get... a table?" I snap back, grabbing a personal pan pizza and putting it on my tray. I walk away quickly so as to delay this conversation.

Five minutes later, I take a seat next to a large window. I have one bite when Jenny and Simone plop down right across from me.

"Okay, we have the table," says Simone. "Now spill. What's the deal?"

"Nothing," I moan.

"You're so snappy and whiny when you have a crush," says Simone. She turns to Jenny and continues, "I like it."

"I'm just happy you're moving on," adds Jenny.

"It's not like that." I mindlessly play with the grease on my paper plate. "I'm just... showing him art techniques."

"Oh? I'm in your class, how come you haven't taught ME these techniques?"

I scowl at Simone. "He's new at this," I deadpan. "And he needs my help."

"Uh huh," grins Simone, pushing up her red-framed classes. "Sure."

"Look we're just friends. And he's... cool to hang out with. He's really easy to talk to. And... "

"And he's hot, I bet," Jenny says.

"He is," adds Simone.

"Okay, okay. Yeah, so what?" I retort, trying not to look them in the eye.

"Look, we're happy you're starting to date again," says Jenny.

"We're not dating."

"But, we just hope you know what you're doing," she continues.

"Going after a straight guy, or a guy who doesn't know what he wants, will never end well," says Simone in a sympathetic tone.

"I know, I know," I want to say, but I think my scowl conveys it, so I take two bites of my pizza and grunt instead. The girls seem to take pity on me as they pivot the conversation to one of Jenny's classes. While I chew, I replay the events of tonight in my head: me, spending time with the most handsome guy I've ever seen, and really, truly connecting with someone for the first time in over a year.

7: Ravi

The next eight days go by in a blur. We hit up The Mousetrap, but Landon and Kareem claim there "aren't enough girls to pull" there, so we call it an early night. Landon makes me swear we'll have a better time next Saturday, so I promise I'll go out again.

In the meantime, when I'm not at art class or on the field, I'm texting Steven pretty regularly. Sometimes he shows me what he's working on. Other times I tell him how annoyingly loud coach was at practice that day. We chat about all sorts of things, make jokes, and send each other hilarious memes. I begin to look forward to our texts and it really feels like we're becoming friends.

Tonight, however, as promised, I'm sitting in a frat house with Kareem, Landon, Omar, and some of the guys on the team (some freshmen, others older). We're in the upstairs kitchen area, sequestered off because Omar is friends with a frat brother, and being on the soccer team certainly gave us that clout on campus. We're sitting around a large, white, all-purpose plastic table, the kind you get at home improvement stores. There's plenty of beer, liquor, and chips around on the countertops.

We sit with a few girls draped around some of the guys-athletics groupies I presume. One girl is behind my chair (Bethany or Brittany or something?) probably trying to get me to notice, but I'm clearly not paying attention to her. Meanwhile, a girl is on Kareem's lap and now there's one on Landon's lap too. Which is the one Kareem has a crush on? I've forgotten since I don't really listen closely to them when they talk about girls.

The thumping music from the floor below fills the room, but we're far enough away that we can actually carry a conversation. Still, we've chosen to play a drinking game, and we all seem to be buzzed and having a good time (better than last weekend anyway).

"Never have I ever…" Landon looks up to ponder. "Gone streaking." A few people laugh as Omar proudly lifts up his cup to take a sip.

"Hey screw you man, you're the one who dared me to do it, you're just trying to get me to drink," replies Omar, smiling.

"Like I need an excuse to do that." Everyone laughs. "Your turn freshman."

"Um," says Paul. "Never have I ever… had a one-night stand." There are approving shouts from all over the room as several guys and girls lift their cups up proudly.

"Now that's something I'll gladly drink to!" Landon laughs. I smile and lift my cup to my lips.

"Ravi, you have?" Kareem asks, pointedly looking at me.

Suddenly all eyes are on me. My face gets warm.

"Uh..." Shit, I was just trying to take a sip.

"I'm sure Ravi-boy is just discrete about it," says Landon, lightly punching me in the shoulder. Fortunately, it seems the heat is off me now. "Okay, okay, your turn freshman." He points at the guy sitting next to Paul.

"Umm.." He looks down at his drink. Vince I think his name was? Fuck I don't remember. "Oh! Never have I ever kissed someone of the same sex!" There's a few murmurs of chuckling and "ooh's" slurred. A couple of the girls drink, gaining the attention of some of the guys. Slowly, Kareem and Landon look at each and share a knowing look.

"OKAY! Okay... technically..." Landon takes a swig. "Kareem and I kissed on a dare."

"That's right you did!" says Omar. He then proudly lifts up his cup to take a dramatic swig.

"You too?" Kareem asks, after putting his cup down.

"Oh no, not on a dare," he says, suggestively winking at all of us. That earns some laughs and buzzes of interest.

"When did YOU do that?" asks Landon, shocked.

"I don't know, a month ago?" shrugs Omar.

"What?!" I ask, incredulously.

"Oh yeah, I hooked up with the guy for a few weeks in the summer." Many jaws drop at Omar's nonchalant confession.

"Are you serious?" Landon asks, now sounding disgusted. I file that away as further evidence as to why I can't come out, not yet.

"It's really not a big deal," giggles Omar.

"No it's not," says the girl sitting in Kareem's lap.

"I actually think it's kinda hot," adds the girl sitting in Landon's lap. Shrugging, she and the other girl clink cups in the air and take a sip. Landon looks at the girls like they've grown three heads.

"What so... so what are you... GAY now?" asks Landon, still dumbfounded.

"No, I still like girls too," says Omar. "I can prove it to you." He winks at the girl sitting on Landon's lap. "Why don't you come give me a kiss, sweetheart?" He gives his thousand-dollar smile.

The girl giggles and blushes and this makes Landon look frustrated. Vince and Paul are still in shock and Kareem just looks amused.

"Okay who's turn is it?" asks Kareem.

"Why aren't we gonna talk about this any more?!" asks Landon.

"Because it's not a big deal," replies Omar. My shoulders relax in relief.

"Not everyone is straight," says one of the girls.

"It's called a spectrum," adds Paul. Vince and some girls nod in agreement. "Gay, bi, pan..."

"Yeah bro, it's just sex," states Omar. "I like having it." He grins, lifting his chin and his red cup up.

"Here here!" adds Kareem, lifting his cup as well. Landon looks around, still confused. Finally, he looks straight at me.

I can't help but chuckle. "Don't look at me man, you're the one who kissed Kareem."

"On a dare!"

"Just drop it." I'm outright giggling now. "It's not a big deal." Landon looks down, confused and defeated.

"Your turn freshman," Kareem says, after a beat of silence.

"Never have I ever..." Paul's eyes light up. "Had two girls kiss me on the cheek at once." That one earns laughter and hollers of approval from everyone, as two girls give each other a knowing look and walk up to him and plant a kiss on

31

his face. I think he'll fit in just fine at college.

—

Two hours later, I'm stumbling out of a cab when I spy the familiar face that's been haunting my dreams for two weeks. Steven and some girls are outside at a wooden table, seemingly packing up a hookah machine. The other guys from the team don't even notice as I leave and walk toward them. My skin feels warm, but I'm riding this buzz while it makes me extra social. I smile a little more and puff up my chest as I approach them. I sure hope Steven likes my smile.

"Hey Steven!"

"Ravi my man!" He walks up to me and gives me a signature side-bro-hug that I hold onto a little bit longer than usual. "What's up?"

"Not much. Just coming back from a party, still feeling... energetic. Felt like being friendly." I giggle and give him a light punch on his shoulder. I have no idea what I'm doing at this point, but he laughs.

"Clearly you've had some libations," chuckles Steven. "It's making you talk much louder than usual."

"Yeah, yeah." I nod, still grinning like an idiot. "I went out with some teammates. Speaking of, coach made us do 20 push-ups yesterday. Wanna watch me do them?" I try to get down on the floor when Steven stops me.

"Hey whoa there cowboy," laughs Steven. "As much as I'd love that, I should help my friends pack up and..." He turns around and sees some of the girls backing away.

"We got this!" says one of them. "You stay. Goodnight Ravi!"

"Night!" I reply. I have no idea who that is. Once they're out of earshot, I whisper to Steven, "I have no idea who that is."

"That's Simone." He giggles. "She's in our art class."

"Right yeah... but I don't KNOW her know her. She's not my art buddy." I smile. Steven giggles. I feel warm. I feel happy.

"Hey, it's getting late, maybe I should walk you to your dorm."

"Mmkay," I mutter, my eyelids getting heavy. "So chivalrous." Steven starts to lead me across the campus road.

My dorm is situated in a small cul-de-sac area, where three other buildings with large windows face inward. The athletics dorm is the newest one and is located right at the top. After a five-minute walk (more of a stumble at times) in silence, I stand in front of my building and pause for a moment.

"Well..." says Steven. Before I lose the courage, I turn and wrap my arms around him, bringing my chin to his shoulder. "Oof," he says.

"Thanks for walking me home," I mutter. "Such a gentleman."

"No problem buddy," Steven chuckles. If I didn't know any better I'd say he sounds uncomfortable, but I don't know why. Without further thought, I immediately turn away, swipe my ID card, and walk quickly into the building.

Once in my room, I strip off my shirt and lie on the bed. I smell the shirt in my hand one more time. Yes, it smells like cheap booze, but it also smells like Steven. I toss it on the floor then fade into sleep, trying to memorize the scent and the way his body fit perfectly wrapped in my arms.

8: Steven

Things were going to get interesting today, Wednesday, in
Prof. Irons' class. Not because I was feeling any weirdness
with Ravi; we acted perfectly casual with each other in class
on Monday. Today, however, we were going to have our first
nude model. When Irons announced that the model would be
arriving earlier in the semester than scheduled, Ravi looked a
little more uncomfortable than usual. I assured him it would
be fine, but I knew today I would need to ease his anxiety
again.

As I go to take my seat, I find Ravi swiveling slowly in his
stool looking down.

"Time for some nudes!" I blurt out.

His eyes go wide. "What?"

"The model," I say, smiling. I guess I should have led with
that.

"Oh right." His eyes dart down again.

"Don't worry. It's usually some stranger you'll never see

again."

"Yeah I hope so." He takes out his paper and charcoal.

"Now class," announces Prof. Irons, gaining our attention. "Be respectful and use the model's time WISELY. We only have her for today's class. She'll sit right here. Come on out then."

A girl about 5-ft.-5 walks in from the closet wearing a grey silk robe. Her make-up is all done up and she looks perfectly curvy like an hour-glass underneath it.

"This is Bethany. Bethany, meet the class."

"Hey class," she greets, confidently. "Hi everyone. Hi Ravi." She smiles and I swear there's a twinkle in her eye as she looks at him.

"Bethany you can disrobe when you're ready and sit right here. Get ready to start everyone, and please remember your sight-lines. Draw them out and erase them later if you need to." As Prof. Irons helps Bethany up to the stool, I turn to Ravi.

"You know her?!" I ask, in a very loud whisper. He looks like he's seen a ghost.

"I uh..." He coughs. "She looks familiar." He proceeds to stare intently at his paper.

Something strange stirs in me at that moment. I turn to look at our model; Bethany is sitting on the stool, now naked and turned away from my side of the studio. From an artist's perspective, she has plenty of interesting curves, and the way the light catches the side of her perky boobs reminds me of classical artists drawing the sun and the moon. From a straight guy's perspective, sure, I can see why Ravi might like her: soda-bottle figure and high cheekbones and all that shit.

But from a human perspective? I'm burning with rage. Is

this the kind of girl that Ravi likes? Did he hook up with her already? Are they gonna like... date and get married and have babies?

I don't know why I'm so annoyed; it's not like I ever had a shot with Ravi. I just... I don't know. I guess I deluded myself into thinking being friends with me would make him not want to hook up with girls. I'm an idiot in that sense.

--

Forty minutes later, I hear Prof. Irons on her phone. "Well I need the water heater TURNED BACK on. No... okay... NO!" she shouts into her cell. "Let me speak to the manager!" She turns to Bethany. "Umm... let's take a break. School policy says we can't have you with no clothes on while I'm not in the room, so please put on your robe. I'll be back in 15 minutes." With that, she helps Bethany get down and leaves the room.

I feel myself acting cold toward Ravi, but I can't get myself to stop.

"Look..." says Ravi, turning to me.

"Hey Ravi!" says Bethany in a cutesy tone. She has her robe back on and has sauntered over to us wearing slippers. "What a CO-INCE this is!" She stands right next to him.

At this point I'm shooting daggers into the table with my eyes. I'm not listening to your girlfriend's conversation Ravi, LA LA LA LA LA.

"Hey," says Ravi unenthusiastically.

"It sucks you had to leave the party so soon last weekend."

"Uh yeah."

"I was trying to text you to hang out, but none of my girls could get your number." Out of the corner of my eye I see her touch his arm lightly.

"Yeah well... I been busy- soccer and all that."

"Even just for a drink? With me?"

Seriously, take a HINT lady.

"Yeah, well I been practicing art a lot... Um I gotta go take a leak, I'll be back." He gets up and I wait three whole seconds before I follow him.

In the hallway, I catch up to him darting to the rest room. "Ravi what was that?"

"Nothing," he says, entering the men's room. "That was nothing."

"Didn't sound like nothing. Did you go out with this girl?" I manage to ask without too much jealousy.

"NO," he immediately replies. "We just met at a party last weekend."

"The night I escorted your drunk ass home?"

"Yeah." He smiles at me. It's quickly replaced with a serious look. "We met but... I'm really not interested."

"Ah." I breathe a sigh of relief.

"Seriously. I'm not."

"Can't keep the ladies away, can ya?" I tease.

Ravi looks relieved. "Fuck out of here." He chuckles.

"Come on, let's go back to class and sketch this girl before Prof. Irons loses her marbles."

"We're way past that," laughs Ravi.

I smile as we walk back to class. The rest of the drawing session I can feel a calmness restored between him and I, and we both manage to get some pretty good sketches of the model before class ends.

—

Saturday mornings are a great time for brunch. They're not, however, a great time for solitude. It seems the entire student body wants French toast as well, because the dining hall

37

nearest to my dorm is jam packed. I somehow manage to find a spot to sit and eat in peace.

I'm sitting at a far table near a window with other couples on both sides of me. I would rather awkwardly sit between two people in silence than try to walk and eat French toast and syrup. Some mornings I just want to be left alone. The universe hears this plea and decides to say *"screw you"* because the next thing I know, all four people next to me finish eating and leave.

"Oh great," I think to myself. *"Now other people are gonna want to sit next to me. As long as they don't try to talk to me, I'll be good."* I look down at my phone with a scowl, giving the universal sign of *"Do NOT approach me"*.

This seals my fate as I feel someone sit, not two chairs away, but right next to me.

"I see you still have a sweet tooth." My pulse quickens as I recognize the voice.

"Sean," I state, trying to maintain neutrality, looking up. I can't deny it: my exboyfriend looks pretty good today. His skin is a bit darker and his brown eyes look as nice as they always have. He seems to have cut his hair and the stubble is working for him. "You're back from Italy."

"Can't study abroad forever." He smiles as he sets his tray of food down and sits next to me. I didn't want him to stay, but whatever. "How's the semester treating you?"

"Good. Yourself?"

"So far no complaints. Classes are rough, but nothing some coffee can't help me with." He smiles. It actually disarms me as I feel myself getting back into the friendly groove that we held for a long time.

"Cool." I proceed to take another bite of French toast loaded with syrup. He never liked how I ate so many sweets, so I'm reveling in it now. "I wish you the best..."

"Don't you have a big exhibition this semester?" he asks.

"Yeah actually." I'm touched to know that he remembers some of my work and my passion. "I'm trying to decide which pieces will make the cut."

"Maybe I can help you," he says with an earnestness I haven't heard in years. "Do you have any pics?"

I wonder if showing him my stuff is too personal. Then I think, 'screw it,' I've never feel uncomfortable showing people my finished works, and it's not like Sean is a stranger; we once a shared a significant part of our lives together. I pull out my phone and open up the album with photos of my recent work.

"Oh, I really like this one," he remarks looking down at my phone. "I've always been a sucker for surrealism." He swipes through. "Wow, you've grown a lot as an artist."

"Thanks," I reply, leaning in to see the phone. I feel myself blush. I like flattery, what can I say?

As he continues to scroll, I look at his face. For a moment, it feels like Sean and I still have something. It's a brief flash of memory, but I snap out of it. I realize confidently that we're, at best, old friends, and not lovers. He's definitely not someone I want to pursue.

9: Ravi

10 o'clock in the morning is TOO early to be this pissed. Yet here I am, aimlessly smashing my scrambled eggs with a fork at the dining hall. Everyone knows this is the best time and place for brunch, and most of us in the athletics dorms can't stop eating.

I'm sitting here with my friends/suitemates at a large table on the side. It's pretty crowded, but we got here early enough. This is a pretty standard weekend morning: I'm eating breakfast, Omar is drinking coffee nursing a hangover, Landon is talking about some girl he's texting, and Kareem is nodding politely, because we all know he's the only one who consistently has girls overnight. This is all very predictable, and because of that, I find comfort in my friends.

However, what's getting me livid this morning is about three tables ahead of me. Through the crowds, I saw Steven sit down about five minutes ago. He looked so cute tired, it made me smile. It was the highlight of my morning, until some guy decided to show up and be all friendly with him.

Now I'm glaring right at them, and through the crowded dining hall, no one seems to notice. Some (admittedly handsome) guy is currently sitting way too close to Steven while they scroll through his phone. He's got well-styled black hair, a fresh tan, a tight black wool shirt, and has like, four rings per hand. They're looking through Steven's phone, exchanging fond glances, and talking excitedly. Everything about this random man screams queer, and, not only that, he seems to be flirting like crazy. Steven doesn't even notice when they guy's chest slightly grazes his shoulder.

Seriously, WHO IS THIS GUY? And why are they smiling so much? And why is my pulse racing?

Maybe, Steven is being too polite and this guy is being a creep. Maybe... maybe I should go in there and save him. Yeah.

I take one last stab at my eggs, then get up.

"You done?" asks Landon.

"Um, yeah. You guys stay. I... have diarrhea."

"Ew," Landon replies and Kareem makes a face.

"See you later," I say without even looking again. In one motion I toss out my food and walk through the aisles, past three other tables.

I'm finally standing right next to Steven and he hasn't even noticed me because *Mr. Wears-too-many-rings* is laughing in his ear. I hear him say, "Yeah you should definitely fly out there some time." His voice is annoying. "Uhh... hi?" Now he's looking up at me.

"Where are we flying?" I ask, my face trying to be neutral. Steven turns around in surprise.

"Oh hey man what's up?" He smiles at me. I immediately feel the anger slip away when he looks into my eyes.

"Hey, hey, how's it going, how are we all doing here?" I ask

41

rhetorically, trying to sound cordial.

"I'm fine, me and Sean were just uh, catching up."

"Cool."

At this point Sean chimes in. "Yeah, Steven and I go way back. He and I are kind of ...together romantically..." My heart stops beating at his words. Steven looks at me mortified and turns around. "...and then we're not... and then we are... and then we're not!" chuckles Sean.

"Okay, we definitely are NOT, haha..." adds Steven. His laughter sounds so forced. His eyes are starting to bug out, but it calms me down to know that this Sean guy is talking out of his ass. "Seriously we're just... old friends."

"Until we're not!" Sean laughs, refusing to interpret Steven's tone. "On again, then off... it's a cycle."

A cycle with no wheels, seems like it.

"It's... not..." Steven stammers with an awkward smile. He looks like he'll throw up at any moment. His eyes reach mine, wide and desperate, almost as if to say *"don't listen to him."*

It's decided then: I need to get Steven as far away from this guy as possible. Time to put my plan into action. "So you ready to get going Steven? You promised to show me some techniques in the studio after breakfast?"

"Uhh... " He stares at me perplexed for a moment until he finally gets it. "Yes! Yes." He turns to Sean. "Gotta run."

"Of course," Sean replies. "Gotta keep working on your craft. Nice meeting you..." He tries to get me to say my name, but I decide to be petty while Steven gets up.

"Nice to meet you too!" I announce and the two of us quickly make an exit.

--

Once outside, I can barely keep up with Steven's power-walk pacing away from the dining hall. Is he the soccer player here? I can feel a mess of nerves emanating from him, unlike the calm demeanor I'm so used to by now.

"Slow down man, I think we're free," I say, trying to lighten the mood. "We made our getaway."

"What the fuck is up with Sean?! Ugh, I can't believe he said that!" Steven barks, looking down, while still not slowing his walk. I think he's talking to himself at this point. "Who does he think he IS saying any of that? He's such a... "

With this he finally looks up at me. His brow is furrowed and he sounds out of breath when he continues, "I'm sorry you had to hear that. He's not my boyfriend. And we're not '*on and off*', whatever that means." He shakes his head.

At this point we're almost halfway across the quad. "Hey, listen," I say. I put my hand on his shoulder to get his attention (I may let it linger there for a moment too long, but no one's around, so I let myself indulge). He finally stops and turns to me, but refuses to make eye contact. "It's okay Steven. I get it. And he's not here."

This seems to snap him out of it and he finally looks at me. The usually curious glint in his eyes is replaced with vulnerability, and I'm not sure which one I find more attractive. "You don't have to explain anything to me," I add. "I got you."

"You helped me make a getaway." He finally starts to grin.

"Yes." I smile. "And now you are free to go about your day." His shoulders starts to relax, and it feels good knowing that I contributed to that.

"Didn't I say I was going to show you some techniques in the studio?" His tone has a teasing edge.

"Dude, I said that," I reply, visibly confused. "And it was just a lie to get you out of there."

43

"Oh, no, I think it was the truth." Now he has a full on mischievous grin.

"What?"

"Come on," he giggles. "Follow me to the studio, soccer captain." He taps my arms and proceeds to walk away.

"I'm co-captain," I mutter, rolling my eyes. I might sound scared or reluctant, but the truth is, I'm intrigued. Steven has yet to lead me astray, and at this point, frankly, I'm charmed by nearly everything about him.

I am definitely in trouble.

"Oh? Tell me about your co-captain," he says while we walk up the stairs past a grassy knoll.

"Well his name is Kareem. He's one of my best friends and suitemates."

"Really?"

"Yeah I tend to only hang out with guys I live and practice with."

"Jock dorm?"

"Jock dorm," I reply with a smile.

I spend the next five minutes walking to the arts building, answering all of Steven's questions about my teammates / friends. I find that Steven's so easy to talk to, no matter the situation. I just hope one day I have the courage to tell him all about who I really am, and what my intentions are with him (baby steps though).

We finally make it to the art studio. "Isn't it closed Saturdays?"

"Usually… butttttt…" sings Steven while reaching the top of a nearby stack of crates in a dark corner. "Deirdre needed me to get some pieces out of the studio and drag them to an exhibition hall last semester. She showed me where she keeps her emergency spare." He smiles a wicked grin, raising an eyebrow at me while holding up the key.

"Uhh, are we going to get in trouble?" I ask, amused, while he unlocks the door.

"Doubt it. Deirdre loves me, remember?" He opens the door and we walk in.

The room has sunlight blazing through the windows as usual, but there's a different energy now that it's a weekend. It's quieter, and as the door closes behind me, I'm acutely aware that Steven and I are alone. I'm tempted to make a move, or hope he makes a move, when I turn around and see him place several large parchments on the front table. Drawing, art class- right, right. That's why I'm here.

"I'm gonna get some focused sketching done on some of this." He points with his charcoal stylus toward the still-life set-up that Irons has up, even on the weekends. "You can do the same. If you want." I smile and nod, taking the stool next to him.

--

We spend the next hour drawing in silence. After a few minutes, I get really lost in my own work, and I nearly forget that Steven is even there. I understand now how good artists can really lose track of time. I end up making various sketches: some are decent, some look awful, but each time I feel like I'm getting closer to creating the kind of lines and shadings I want.

When I feel like I'm done for the day, I look up and see him packing up. He has an easy smile as he looks over at me. "You all set?"

"Yeah." I get up and return a smile while I wrap up my sketches with a rubber band. "I got some good work done, I think."

"That's great." His smile falters. "I feel like I was supposed to show you techniques or something."

"Don't sweat it."

"I just..." He looks down. "I'm so used to like... working alone on Saturday mornings. It's my time to like..."

"Get away from it all?"

"Yes! Even with my friends or Prof. Irons, just working near them feels like I have to be some form of entertainment, or a star pupil or some shit."

"Putting on a show."

"Exactly! This was probably my first time working with someone in..." He pauses to look down. "A comfortable silence. You're the first who..." He trails off then looks up at me, seriously. "Well I got some work done, so that's great."

I feel a blush taking over my face and smile. "Glad you could. Me too." I hear my inner voice yell, *"Just TELL him you feel comfortable with him too! Tell him you're gay! Tell him you want him!"* I say nothing and we nod in silence.

He looks down and digs his shoe into the floor a little bit. Did his face get redder? "Well, I better go lock up." He proceeds to walk out the door, and I follow. "I don't wanna keep you from your soccer friends, or from your nude-model-groupies or whatever," he teases with a grin.

I laugh. "Hey, the dozens of nude soccer groupies can wait, I'm hanging out with you right now."

He laughs then places the key back on top of the stack where he got it. "Sure buddy." With that, and a wave, he quickly runs down a back staircase, yelling "See you on Monday!"

I'm left standing there alone, stunned at how quickly he got away.

10: Steven

I have the same recurring dream nearly every night, and sometimes during my waking hours: I'm with Ravi in the art studio and he's kissing me. His big strong arms are holding me while his warm torso pushes me until my back touches the drawing table. Pulling back, I look at him intently. Even in my dreams I've memorized his face. He's a world of warm dark skin and loving eyes. I kiss him again, and I can't get enough. His lips are soft-no, rough.

After feeling his tongue explore my mouth, we break apart again and he pulls the bottom of my shirt off, then I finally pull off his and now we're- well, I'm awake.

That's how most of my dreams have been going recently. I wake up sad, frustrated, harder down there than a brick in winter, but most of all, lonely. Catching up with Sean again made me realize that I hadn't really moved on from him.

Did I want him back? Hell no. After the territorial speech he gave Ravi at breakfast, my desire to no longer be with him was cemented. Still, I've been throwing myself into my art and schoolwork so much that I haven't bothered to hook up or date anyone in almost a year.

Now here I was, lusting after Ravi: beautiful, ostensibly straight, confusing Ravi. It was all fun and games when he was just cute eye candy in art class, but now things were different. He saved me from Sean. He calmed me down. He's sweet and genuine, and getting texts from him brightens my day.

I can't shake this feeling that there might actually be something substantial there, but all he does is confuse me. Some days it feels like he wants me, like when we worked together in the studio alone. Then other days all I can think of is nude model girls throwing themselves at him. He says he wasn't into Bethany, but he hasn't made it that clear that he's into me either. It's intruding thoughts like these that made me run away from him last Saturday; I couldn't bear hanging out with him, trying to figure out if he wants me as more than a friend.

I put my pillow in my face and groan in frustration as I wait for my morning wood to go down. No wonder I've avoided dating for so long- this shit is difficult and annoying. I take a deep breath. Then I take another. I blindly reach for my phone and proceed to text Simone.

Me: I need to do something fun, a distraction today.

Me: Yes, this is me cashing in the IOU for all the times I drove your drunk ass home.

Simone: Wow, So pushy on a Wednesday morning. (winky face emoji)

Me: Wasn't there a new restaurant downtown u wanted to go to?

Simone: Yeah, the sushi burrito place.

Me: Let's go early at like 430. Skip art class.

Simone: Playing hooky?

Me: Please. U can mock me later just promise me ull go? I need this.
(sad face emoji)

Simone: Ok yeah.

Feeling satisfied that I've expressed my desperation, I get up and go to the bathroom to start my day.

--

Later that afternoon, I'm halfway through my Japanese beer when Simone points at me with her chopsticks. "Your food's getting cold."

"It's sushi," I retort flatly, wiping my mouth on the back of my hand.

"Okay, well then your food's getting warm."

I smirk. I pick up the sushi burrito and take a big bite. The rice is still cold but the salmon inside is slightly warm; it's gingery, salty, and delicious.

"Have you eaten at all today?" Simone asks, amused.

"No," I mumble with my mouth full while taking another bite.

"Beer, barely eating, playing hooky… what's this all about man?"

My face turns sour as I proceed to engulf the only calories I've had all day.

"You're scaring me, Steven. What's going on?"

"I think you know."

"I do?"

Just then I see a flash on my phone. Think of the devil- Ravi is texting me. "It's Ravi," I inform Simone.

Ravi: Missed u in art today. Playing hooky or sicky?

Me: R u gonna tattle to Irons?

Ravi: I thought u didn't have to be here for elective?

Me: Uve been paying attention to me? LOL

Ravi: Well I did miss u today.

Something warms my stomach upon reading this, and it's not just the beer.

"What's going on?" Simone asks softly, as she finishes her last chunk of rice.

I roll my eyes. "Let's get this over with." I hand over my phone and show her the last four texts.

"Aww!" squeals Simone. "He misses you!"

"Doubt it. He's on the soccer team, they're all straight, remember? He doesn't like me like that."

"And you like him."

"That's why I'm here, avoiding Irons' class, eating my feelings." I angrily take another bite of my burrito.

Just then, Simone's eyes light up as she looks at my phone. "He just texted you!" I nearly knock over my beer to reach my phone.

Ravi: Our first really important game of the season is tonight. I was going to invite you in person.

Ravi: But if ur not feeling well I understand.

My eyes are blown wide. My pulse quickens as I type back.

Me: Is it customary to invite people to ur games?

Ravi: I guess, lol (shrugging emoji)

Me: Do u want me to come?

"What is it? The suspense is killing me!" squeals Simone.

"I asked him if he wants me to come to his soccer game." I'm smiling nervously at this point.

"Smooth!" She grins and nods. Then I receive more texts.

Ravi: *I want all my friends to come.*

Ravi: *But all my other friends are on the field. The only one missing is you.*

Ravi: *It would be cool. Again no big deal if you can't or if ur not feeling well.*

Butterflies buzz around my stomach. Did he really invite just me?

Me: *I'm not sick.*

Me: *But I don't do cheering crowds unless I'm specifically wanted there. (winking face emoji)*

Ravi: *I gotta get ready for the game. No phones on the field and that shit.*

Ravi: *But yeah, if u come we can hang out after? U and me? (smiley face)*

Ravi: *Ttyl.*

I'm full blown smiling as I show my phone to Simone. "Aww," coos Simone. "Well what are we sitting here for? Let's get you ready for the ball, Cinderella!"

"It's a soccer game." I roll my eyes and put away my tray.

"Hurry up so you can go put on something nice!" She pushes me out the door, but the butterflies in my stomach are leading me out just as fast.

--

One hour later, we're walking through the gates on the side of the athletics center. I've never been to a soccer game before, but apparently admission is free for all students. The stands aren't too crowded, so Simone and I are able to get seats up front. The music is blaring some pre-game techno beats to hype up the crowd and I'm so nervous I can barely sit still. After a long 10 minutes, the players finally make it onto the field to bump fists with each other as some sort of pre-game ritual of cordiality.

Ravi, being co-captain, leads the way, so I spot him instantly, tapping fists with each member of the visiting team. I would like to point out one thing: DAMN he looks good in his soccer uniform. Why have I not looked up how he looks in his gear? His shirt hugs him in just the right way accenting his shoulders. His legs are so toned. Most importantly, he looks so energized and confident.

Oh great, now I can expect soccer cleats in all my jerk-off fantasies from now on.

The first half goes by in a blur. Ravi has a lot of time on the field, so he doesn't seem to notice us. The crowd goes wild when he passes to his teammate to score early on, but this wave of energy doesn't last long as the opposing team scores not long after.

At one point, he's on the sidelines and a coach gives him a cup of water. He gulps some of it down, then drenches himself in it. I've never been one to lust after jocks, but good lord, the way he looks with water splashed on him is the stuff of legends. How does this guy keep getting sexier?

After the halftime break is over, Ravi finally spots us. His eyes shine as he nods right at me. I'm aware there are others in the crowd, but there's a look of surprise and familiarity that crosses his face and it doesn't fade away even as he takes the field again. Everything about his vibe while playing is fascinating and beautiful. He's so comfortable in a way I never get to see: he's focused, energetic, and composed. Even the way he dribbles the ball at his feet is sexy.

With two minutes to go, his teammate passes to him and Ravi manages around the opposing players and scores, breaking the tie. For the next three minutes, the crowd is roaring, but I swear, it feels like I'm cheering louder than all of them.

--

Twenty minutes after the game ends, we're waiting outside the men's locker room area, along with some family members. As the players begin to exit, I'm anxiously looking at each person, waiting for the one face I've been dreaming of for weeks.

"Hey!" I hear Ravi before I see him. My eyebrows jump and my smile widens when he finally approaches. He's wearing a track suit with the Korham University logo on it and a matching duffel bag slung over his shoulder. His hair is damp from the shower and as he gets closer I have to resist the urge to run my hands through it. He looks sexy as hell, and I'm officially convinced he can wear any outfit and be the hottest man in the room.

"You made it," he says, with a joy I've never heard from him. We do the awkward fist bump guys do while I try not to read too much into the tone of this voice.

"Ravi! You were incredible out there."

"Thanks."

"You really were," adds an older couple standing near me, while some others next to them agree and nod. Ravi humbly thanks them all with a wave. This man is like a celebrity and I try not to get too jealous at the thought of sharing his attention with anyone.

He taps my shoulder to get me to start walking away from the crowds. "Did you enjoy it?" he asks. He's so genuine, I think he really needs to make sure that I had a good time.

"I did, I did!" I reply, nodding at the ground. "Um, we did!" I add, remembering that Simone is next to me. "You remember Simone right?"

"Oh hey!" he smiles at her.

"Hey Ravi, great game!" The three of us are walking pretty quickly up the sidewalk toward the center of campus.

"So you said you wanted to hang out after the game?" I ask.

"Yeah sure. Maybe we can get food or something."

"You sure you're not tired?"

"Nah man, the buzz I get after a game doesn't wear off for a while."

"Okay. Late night dining hall?"

"Sure." After a moment of walking, he adds, "I'm really glad you made it to the game... Both of you," He's pointedly looking past me at Simone.

"You rocked it, and I don't even like sports!" chimes Simone.

"I had a lot of fun, for real." I smile.

As we're approaching the dining hall, Simone suddenly exclaims, "Oh crap!"

"What?" I ask.

"I promised my mom I'd Skype her so we can talk about that new Korean drama on Netflix."

"Oh umm..." I reply, puzzled.

"I'm so sorry. You guys have fun without me, I gotta run!" She says pointing at both of us. With that, she dashes away into the night. I'm going to have to thank her later for her not-so-subtle attempt to wingman for me.

--

After we get our food, Ravi and I manage to find a corner table far from everyone else in the dining hall. Late night dining has its own section because there are a lot less people and the food is more expensive.

"I'm sorry for abandoning you in art class today," I confess, playing with the straw on my smoothie.

"You should be!" Ravi grins at me. He's got a plate filled with fried carbs with cheese (typical athletes).

"Well someone's sassy." I smirk at him. "This is because you won the game, Soccer Captain."

"Hey, I'm just confident in my ability to play." He shrugs and eats another French fry, oozing athletic cockiness.

"Am I going to have to put up with this for the rest of the year?" I say taking another sip.

For a fleeting moment, something soft flashes in Ravi's eyes. He looks down for a second, and then looks back up at me. The cocky glint in his eye has returned. "Only for the rest of the season."

I chuckle. "Seriously though, you were awesome out there. So confident!"

"Not as confident as you are when you're in the studio, or when you're showing me all the cool techniques you've learned."

"But that's me alone, that's not like, me being surrounded by what feels like the entire school."

"It wasn't that many people."

"Dude, I waited outside next to what felt like the 'Ravi Metta fan club.'" At that we both giggle.

He pauses for a moment and looks down at my hand. "How long have you had this?" Ravi taps the rainbow bracelet on my wrist. His hand grazes mine for a moment and I feel an unseen spark between us.

"Oh this?" I ask lifting it up. "I got it at one of the pride events on campus last year, thought it looked dope." Ravi nods. "Plus I wanna make it extra clear that I'm gay, in case any girls get any funny ideas."

Ravi chuckles for a moment. "How long have you been out?"

"Since I was thirteen." I shrug.

"Wow," replies Ravi, smiling. "That's awesome."

"It's not so awesome when you're a chubby 13-year-old, but when you grow up to be as cool as I am, you can't hide who you are." I smile at him and look up, boastfully.

"I just wish I could be like that," he muses, wistfully looking down. My expression turns serious. What did he mean?

"Ravi, what-" I'm interrupted by Ravi looking up above my shoulder, mortified.

"So this you studying, huh?" One of the other soccer players has approached. He's trailed by another guy who was on the field tonight. They're both wearing the same track suit as Ravi. "You blowing us off now?"

"Uhh no it's not like that," replies Ravi nervously. I look up at his blonde friend who looks down at me. His expression reads as half-amused and half-unimpressed.

"You said you needed to study for a business class and that's why you darted out of the locker room."

"Uh... I didn't wanna go to the Mousetrap. You guys said you were going out. Um, I wasn't in the mood. Why haven't you left yet?"

"We changed our minds," adds his other friend. This one is taller, leaner, with kinder eyes. "It's a school night. So we're gonna be good little undergrad students and play Mario Kart."

"While taking shots," adds the first friend.

"Yup." The second friend smiles. "If you don't come in first place, you take a shot, BUT if you use a blue shell, you take two MORE shots." They both giggle at this.

"We thought we'd get some food beforehand." His blonde friend looks at me again. "What's going on here?" He points between the two of us.

"Hi," I finally interject. "I'm Steven."

"We take art together." Ravi sounds anxious at this point, like he's been taken completely off guard.

"YOU'RE the art guy?" asks the first friend.

"Woah," adds the second friend. "Sorry, you're just… WAY better-looking than I thought you'd be."

My eyebrows shoot up. "Thank you?" I ask with an uncomfortable smile. I'm choosing to move past that comment.

"Mind if we join you?" asks the first friend, staring at Ravi. His tone is accusatory, but I'm not sure what he'd be accusing us of.

"Uhh.." says Ravi.

"We don't mind!" I reply. "It's not like this is a date or anything." I immediately scoot over.

"Bet!" says the blonde one as he sit next to me and immediately steals a French fry from Ravi's plate. "Why aren't you introducing us?"

"That's Landon." Ravi points to the guy who is now sitting next to him and adds, "And this is Omar."

"I'm Steven… again. I was at the game today, you guys were awesome."

"You're just saying that to flatter us 'cause I said you were good-looking," says Omar, smiling and taking a French fry from Ravi.

"While that's certainly welcome," I chuckle, ignoring the blush on my face. "I really meant it. I had fun."

"Are you a fan of sports?" asks Landon. Why do I feel like I'm being interrogated?

"Not really."

"Oof, you're breaking his heart," Omar replies, patting Ravi on the chest. He turns and gives Omar an angry glare. "Our hearts. You're breaking OUR hearts." With that, Landon and Omar giggle.

That's how we spend the next few minutes. Landon and Omar ask me a few more harmless questions, but the conversation eventually turns to the soccer game. They're talking about close calls, and what they wish certain teammates had done better.

Ravi seems to relax as the conversation steers towards something he has major stakes in. I wonder if I could ever get him to talk to me that way. As if hearing my thoughts, he looks at me, but I quickly look down. It feels apparent that I can't add anything to the conversation, so I'm starting to feel a little unwelcome.

After Landon gets up to go to the bathroom, I make up some excuse about being tired and make my exit. I walk quickly, hoping Ravi is watching me go, but not daring to look back to see his face.

Walking outside, I replay today's events over in my head. I dwell on the highs of seeing Ravi in action, and the lows of feeling like he doesn't quite know if he likes me or not. Swiping my ID card and entering my dorm, I resolve to not think about it for the rest of the night. I need to refocus my efforts on my semester exhibition. I need to forget about this stupid crush on Ravi. I can totally tamp down these feelings.

Maybe, if I say that lie enough, it will become true.

11: Ravi

For the next seven days, I can feel Steven slipping away from me. We used to have witty rapport in class, but now that's changed. He's not really icing me out, but he's so hyper-focused on his piece in class on Monday that I can barely talk to him. We used to chat (and possibly flirt?) all about our day when we weren't together, but now I'm getting one-word answers and texts hours later.

It's been a week since Landon and Omar crashed my after-game dinner session with Steven, and I'm still kind of pissed about it. Things were going so well after the game, but he basically ran away screaming when the guys showed up. I can't say I blame him; Landon isn't exactly easy to get along with sometimes and all they did was get me to talk about soccer. What was with Omar's flirting? I can't seem to wrap my head around any of it.

"It's not like this is a date."

Steven's words have been echoing in my head. Those

seven little words shot down all of my romantic fantasies. I wanted to reply, *"It could be! Let's go on a date right now and leave these losers!"* but of course I said nothing like the coward I am.

Today, I'm waiting in my usual seat in art class, and almost everyone is here, except for the big empty stool next to mine. One minute before class officially starts, I spot Steven walking in. He's got his traditional beanie and the eyebrow piecing I like. Today he's wearing a white hoodie, which is baggy compared to the skinny jeans on his legs. He looks perfect.

He sits next to me and I muster up my cheeriest version of "Hey man! How's it going?" That sounded so generic, I feel like an idiot.

"I'm good," he replies, taking out his sketchbook. "How'd your away game go?"

"We actually won. 2-to-1 again."

"Nice, nice. You score the winning goal again?"

"No, I did the assist though. Landon got it."

"Ah." I notice his eyes start to move down and his interest fade. I need to make this right.

"Listen, about last week, the guys-"

CLAPCLAPCLAP.

Prof. Irons is once again waving her plastic clapper. "Attention! Attention class!"

I have to stop talking and everyone in the class does as well. I really want to continue our conversation, but that just isn't happening now.

"Today we'll be starting to make our own ink for the etching portion of the semester. This is, after all, Drawing and *INKING* 101," shouts Prof. Irons. "It can't just be all charcoal sketching and nude models."

"Aww, but think of all the learning that can be done from nudes!" proclaims Steven, prompting laughter from the whole class.

"Mr. O'Rourke, since you want to be the peanut gallery, you'll be my inking guinea pig."

"You're just picking on me 'cause I did this like 20 times last semester," says Steven, walking up to the designated ink station on the side of the studio.

"Exactly. You'll be demonstrating the process of making black ink for etching."

"Alright, alright." He turns for a quick moment, then dashes back to his seat next to mine. "Almost forgot." He immediately unzips his white hoodie and places it on a window sill. "Don't wanna get too much of a stain on it."

Taking off his hoodie, Steven reveals a world of skin, previously unseen by me. He's wearing a tight blank tank top that is stuck to his body perfectly, leaving almost nothing to the imagination. His deltoids are protruding and his abs are showing through the thin fabric.

Fuck. Fuuuuck.

My brain has stopped functioning with all my blood rushing down south.

How can I concentrate on anything Irons is saying with Steven wearing so little clothing and class is requiring me to stare at him?

He picks up some powder and makes a small pile on the inking table. Irons says something about it being flammable, and I'm trying to listen to the instructions, but I don't think my ear drums have any nerves or blood right now. My eyes are using all of my energy soaking in the sight of Steven as he proceeds to pour some thick liquid on the powder. Now he's taking some utensil that looks like an ice scraper and is using it to crush the powder into the liquid. His biceps and deltoids bulge and pop in all the perfect ways as he presses and crunches. He's looking down concentrating, and his wrists clench as the powder turns into a glob of ink.

I'm so turned on right now I can barely breathe. I didn't know 'Drawing and Inking 101' would be some sort of erotic fantasy of mine, but here we are.

--

Sometime later, we split up into groups: some folks start making ink with the assistance of Steven, while others, including myself, sketch their future projects. I am in the unfortunate situation of sitting near the inking station, so Steven's perfectly formed arms and sexy torso are on constant display to me. I don't know if I should cheer or cry about this.

Five minutes into attempting to sketch, I hear someone sit next to me. "You doing alright Ravi?" I'm brought back to reality by the sound of Simone's voice.

"Um yeah. Why wouldn't I be?"

"You just look uncomfortable. Or distracted..." she remarks, voice heavy with implication. Her eyes dart between me and Steven, but behind her red-rimmed glasses, she looks inquisitive, yet not judgmental.

"Distracted?"

"By the difficulties of inking... right?"

"Right," I reply, hoping it doesn't sound like a lie. I look down at my sketch like it's the most interesting thing in the world. After a heavy pause, she continues.

"You know, Steven and I have been good friends for awhile."

"Oh?" My eyes refuse to look at her, but I need her to

continue talking. Where is she going with this?

"He's a really good guy. He's fun, he's sweet, he knows when to shut up, and he knows when to make people laugh."

I look around to make sure no one is within ear shot. "I know. We've been… hanging out."

"Well the look on your face and the sour mood he's constantly in makes me feel like you two haven't… officially…"

My face gets warm while I look at my sketch. I draw some arbitrary lines as my heart beats out of my chest. There's no point in hiding it at this point. "We're just friends. We haven't… done anything."

"I'm not gonna say anything! Almost everyone in my circle is um, queer, and it's not a big deal."

I have no idea how to respond to any of this. "Okay."

"I just don't want to see my good friend get hurt." Her tone conveys sincerity and tenderness. No wonder Steven trusts her.

"I wouldn't do that." With that I look up at Steven. He's smiling while some girl manages to make a massive glob of ink. There's a twinkle of pride on his face as he moves to help someone else start the process. "Besides, he's made it clear he wants to be just friends."

"Did you ask him out? Like on a real date?" Simone whispers.

"Well…" I pause and look up at her. "Not officially, no." I sound like an idiot, but maybe this time I am.

"You boys are so…" She rolls her eyes and smiles. "You're the captain of the soccer team. You really think he'd turn you down?"

"Co-captain."

"Who cares? Dude, just make a move."

"What if I'm not like... ready to..."

"Not ready... to go public?" I shrug in response. "Then leave him alone... OR you two can STOP being so damn miserable and kiss already."

With that she walks away, and others start to move back to the rest of the classroom, much closer to my seat. I see Steven by the sink washing his hands. He dries his hands on a paper towel then uses it to wipe his face.

When he's concentrating on art, when he's helping others, and even when he's just talking to me, Steven is majestic. Simone's words have given me a lot to think about. Coming out is scary, but I just can't leave him alone.

I'm out of my element all the time when I'm around him, but I need to shoot my shot- one way or another.

--

Friday night I decide to text him.

Me: Wut r u doing tomorrow afternoon?

Steven: Nothing, I think.

Me: Wanna break into the studio to get some work done?

Steven: Break in? Ur naughty. (smiley face emoji)

Me: Hey u started it. Ur a bad influence on me. (winky face emoji)

Steven: I am behind on figures for my portfolio.

Me: I'll meet u there at 12.

Steven: I never agreed!

Me: U really gonna say no to me?

Steven: I've corrupted u. Cyu then.

--

The next afternoon I meet him at room 311. After he greets me, he gets the spare key again from the stack of crates and opens the studio. We exchange pleasantries while setting up. In the center of the classroom is the still-life of the week: this time it's some cardboard cut into geometric shapes, all about two-feet tall. In front of them is the stool, commonly used by models.

We get to work in silence and my heart is pounding the whole time. The air is thrumming with tension. All I'm thinking about is how alone we are here, and how I really want to make a move. I'm so nervous I'm actually starting to sweat. Did it get hotter in here?

"Um," I cough. "I'm sorry about my friends." He looks up at me, puzzled. "From the other day? When they crashed our... us at the dining hall."

"It's cool. They weren't intruding on anything, so..." His voice trails off and he shrugs. He immediately goes back to rifling through his sketches. His complete apathy is killing me. I thought I had a shot, why is he being so distant?

Maybe I should just nut up and tell him I'm gay too, or even better tell him I like him. *"Just ask him out!"* screams the voice in my head. *"For real, on a date! Or better yet, kiss him now!"* I end up doing neither of these.

"Hey Steven?" I ask, not sure where I'm going with this.

"Yeah?- aw fuck!" he barks, barely paying attention to me, but instead, sifting through various pages in his sketch book. "Fuck."

"What's wrong?"

"I'm supposed to have at least one more decent full body sketch for my portfolio assignment in my advanced fine arts class." He pulls out a paper that looks like a syllabus. Then, he puts it down and flips to a previous page in his book. The page has a complete nude model sketch of a girl about our age, but the face is blurred with purposeful shadow. The rest of the body looks so real, like a phantom that could leap out at any moment; Steven's work never ceases to amaze me.

"Wow that's awesome."

"Yeah, but what's NOT awesome is my professor reaming me for turning in an incomplete assignment, AGAIN." He looks down and runs his fingers through his hair, clearly still frustrated. "She told me it's bad enough I'm spending so much time in DI101 that..." He looks up at me briefly, then back down. "Well it doesn't matter."

"What can you do?"

"Nothing. Well I guess I can find something off the internet to sketch, but it's never quite the same as the real deal."

Perfect, now's my chance. My heart is thrumming loudly as I stand up. "Maybe I can help," I state nonchalantly. I don't want to overthink this, or I'll chicken out.

"How?" Steven asks as I walk to the front of the room. I lock the door, and the energy in the room immediately changes.

"How about I be your nude model?" I ask, walking up to the stool.

"Wha... Wha... What?" he asks, his eyebrows flying up and his jaw dropping.

I strip off my shirt and toss it beside me. I swear I hear a small gasp from Steven, and his eyes are huge right now. He's only about three feet in front of me, but I feel the heat coming off him; I want him to feel the heat off of me.

"Well? You said you need the real deal." I unbuckle my belt. I do it extra slowly while his eyes dart from my crotch to my abs. His mouth is still hung open. Yes, I'm teasing him- I want him to want me. "I'll be your model." With a swift motion I pull my jeans down to my ankles and sit on the bench. I'm wearing black briefs (I may have worn my fanciest pair just in case of this exact scenario) and the bench feels cold on my bare thighs, but I don't care.

How can I focus on anything with Steven's gaze roaming

over my legs, crotch, and abs, darting up and down.

"Well?" I ask again, raising an eyebrow for emphasis.

"You...uh. Uh. Uh...You." He's stammering like a broken record.

"You're right. Irons said we can't be nude unless the professor is in the room, so I'll just have to be down to my briefs, if that's alright."

"Uh..Uh...Uh..." His eyes are still blown wide and his mouth opens and closes like a fish out of water; I'll take that as a sign he's enjoying this show I'm putting on. I swear he hasn't blinked in like 45 seconds.

"Come on man. I'm your model. Let's do this." I make my voice sound extra husky for that last bit. Being the athlete that I am, I'm always concerned about fitness, but rarely do I appreciate my form. This morning, however, I took extra care to do some push-ups and sit-ups, so my abs are especially bulgy today.

Judging by the wide-eyed expression and lack of words from Steven, I'd say my physique is thoroughly appreciated right about now.

"You should probably get on that."

"What?!" he yelps, finally blinking and shaking his head.

"Your assignment. Get on that."

"Oh. Right." He finally puts his charcoal stylus to the paper and begins some strokes.

After a few moments I decide to push him a little further. "Is this a good pose? Do you want me in a different position?" His eyebrows jump, but he says nothing while he sketches. "Do you want me from behind?"

"NOPE!" he squeaks. "THIS IS..." He coughs and brings his voice back down an octave. "This uh.. this works."

"Alright." I smile. I feel a little guilty playing with my

words like that, but I want him to like me. I want him to think I'm sexy, even if that means putting some naughty thoughts into his head.

After four more minutes, he says, "This is um... really good stuff. Good subject matter."

"Yeah?"

"Yeah, I've never drawn anyone with um... yo-your... bo-bo-bo-body." His face is cherry red now, and he's refusing to look directly at me. I've never heard him stutter before. It's adorable, especially since I'm the one doing this to him. I think it's time I put him out of his misery.

"Look Steven, if you're free, I was hoping we could... ya know."

"We could what?" he asks, still not looking at me.

"Go out." I look up, my heart pounding in my ears.

"What do you mean?" He sounds genuinely confused. How am I fumbling this? "Out to where?"

"Go out. Just the two of us."

"That sounds like date," he scoffs, his face turning redder.

"Well... yeah," I state. He finally looks me in the eyes. "A date. 'Cause... I like you." Upon hearing this, his expression softens and his eyes stare directly into my soul. "And-"

Before I can continue, I hear the familiar clicking of the door unlocking.

In one swift ninja maneuver, I pull up my pants and grab my shirt from the ground, then dash across the room to behind the inking table. I hear Steven scramble to put away his papers while the distinct sound of Prof. Irons' voice booms through the room.

"NO... BUT NO.... I DID pay the water bill. I paid it ALREADY. But... NO." She's clearly on the phone. I can't confirm because I'm ducking into the utility closet while putting my belt back together. While I put my shirt on I hear them start talking.

"Steven, why are you here?!"

"Deirdre-"

"No HOW are you here?"

"I can explain."

"No WHY are you here in my studio?! It's a Saturday."

"I used the spare key-"

"Dammit I knew I shouldn't have trusted you."

"BUT for a legitimate reason," he claims, exasperated. "Uh, Ravi forgot his sketchbook!"

Now that I'm fully clothed, I use that as my cue. I grab some papers and charcoal from the closet and walk right out, trying to even my breaths. "Found it!" I proclaim.

Prof. Irons looks at me like I'm an idiot. "Look you two can't just- HELLO?" she yells into her phone. "NO. NO I want to speak to a REPRESENTATIVE." She glares at the two of us and points to the door. We gather our things and quickly take the exit we're given. By the time we make it down the stairs, we're both giggling a sigh of relief.

As we walk outside, he's outright laughing and I can't help but laugh too. "That was wild."

"I know, I know, jeez," I chuckle.

"WAYYY too close."

"Do you think we'll get in trouble?"

"Nah. I'll just have to find some other times to sneak in." He smiles at me and I return it. Then, I clear my throat. The nerves are sinking in again.

"So um, about that uh, THING we were talking about."

"Yeah," he replies, looking down. He's playing with his shoe on the cement again. "Did you mean to ask me out... like... like on a date?"

"I did."

"And you said you liked me?" He's still looking down.

"I do."

"Are you being for real right now?"

"Yes!"

He finally looks me in the eye. He's gorgeous and endearing and I'd like to keep staring at him whenever I get the chance. Just then, it occurs to me that we're outside, and I look around to see if anyone is listening. The coast is clear, but when I look back at Steven, his eyebrows are furrowed. "I meant what I said."

"But, it looks like you don't want anyone to know." He sounds so defeated.

"I'm just..." I don't know how to finish that sentence.

"No it's cool. I just didn't' know you were, um... " He shakes his hand in front of his head to wipe away an imaginary haze. "Uh. I've just been out... for so long, and this is a lot to process."

"That's fair." I nod and look off to the side. "Are you... um... interested in me?" I sound like a second-grader but I can't help it, I need to know.

When I look at him, I see a shy smile on his face- a good sign? "Look Ravi you're, uh, VERY attractive." Score. I want to pump my fist in the air. "But I-" Oh no.

"But?" I plead.

"You're not out at school are you? With the team or anything. It's not my style to hide who I'm dating. So, I don't know..."

Of course. I'm the closeted idiot asking for so much from him. Why would someone as confident and sexy as Steven want to date a coward like me? "NO it's fine I get it," I say quickly. "Take your time. Think it over. In fact, just uh, table

71

it: take a day- no, take a WEEK!" I'm babbling at this point and I give him two big thumbs up while walking backward; what's wrong with me? "We can... talk some other time. I'll uhh catch ya later."

"Ravi, look, it's not that I don't-"

"Hey I gotta go!" I continue to babble, walking backwards. "I have to go over some drills with some freshmen so uh, text me? I'll see you in class Monday. And uh, peace out!" I'm shouting by the end of this, and I spin around (nearly bumping into a college tour group) and briskly walk away. I don't think I could bear to see the rejection on Steven's face right now.

As pathetic as it was, I gave it my best shot. I can only hope Steven chooses to look past all my baggage and give me a chance.

12: Steven

Monday morning I wake up early from a night of unsatisfactory sleep. Every time I close my eyes, I see Ravi wearing very little clothing. I see his chest, his abs, and his thighs, all of it layered with delicious muscle that I could stare at for days.

"You said you need the real deal. I'll be your model."

The memory of him saying those words while looking me in the eye and taking off his clothes will be forever seared into my brain. When he started his little 'art-school-strip-tease', it felt like a deluge went straight down into my cock. I was so hard by the time he had his jeans down to his ankles, it literally started to hurt.

"A date. 'Cause I like you."

Then he went and said he wants to date me! What game are you playing Ravi Metta?

Oh right, the game I invented the moment I began flirting with him the day we met. In my defense, this was supposed to be harmless flirting; I didn't want a relationship, because history taught me that they could only lead to misery. Now I have this guy (this gorgeous guy who's sweet, but totally closeted) who supposedly likes me and I don't know what to do next.

Fuck, this hard-on is never going to go away is it? I need to get a grip, or get laid, or both.

I get up and go to the bathroom for my morning pee. I use a towel to cover my obvious erection as I walk through the halls to the communal bathroom. I'm not too ashamed because I'm pretty sure all of us guys on this floor cover ourselves in various ways every morning.

Except this time, the reason is clear: when I close my eyes, I see the world of perfect skin and muscled terrain that is the school soccer captain. Mr. Popular-and-Sexy is turning down girls left and right because he says he's gay and he wants me.

Well he never actually said he was gay. Is he? Does he really want to date me? Will we have to hide from his friends? Will I even be able to? If I can't hide it, will they beat me up or something? Am I going to be a victim of a hate crime?

I can't take these questions, and I certainly can't face Ravi in art class today. So, after I get dressed, I shoot Prof. Irons an e-mail and text Simone. Then, I throw a bag into my car and drive off.

--

Three hours later I'm driving up to my childhood home. Since it's only the beginning of fall, the driveway is clear of snow, but I park in the street anyway so as to not to block my mom's car.

I take a deep breath before opening the back door. I walk in hoping to get to my room unnoticed. I'm greeted by the blaring sounds of some cartoon in the living room past the kitchen, where I find various boxes of cereals, macaroni, and fruit snacks scattered about. I walk in a little further to make sure nothing's on fire, and that's when I hear someone coming up the stairs.

"Steven! Honey you're home!" My mom walks in with a laundry basket stuck to her hip.

"Uh yeah, hi Mom-" I'm interrupted with the clamoring of two pairs of little feet.

"Grandma, grandma! Lola broke the pink dolly I was playing with!"

"No I didn't Grandma, Lottie's lying!" My twin five-year-old nieces are running up to my mom, hopping up and down.

"Now girls, if you don't play nice, I'm going to sit you out for quiet reading time again. You don't want that right?" My mom is using the tone I grew very accustomed to growing up, but I can tell she's tired today, and it isn't even 2pm.

"Hey baby girls, you're not gonna greet your favorite uncle?" I say, crouching down.

"Uncle Steve!" They turn and greet me in unison. It's so cute when they do that.

"You're not our favorite uncle, what about Uncle Sly?" Lola asks. At least I'm 90% sure it's Lola.

"He buys us ice cream sometimes but he said only if HE'S our favorite," says Lottie (I assume).

"So we told him we liked him better than you Uncle Steve!"

"But we can change our minds if you buy us some ice cream too!" Lola adds. For two kids who fight a lot, they sure have the twin-telepathy powers down.

"Uhh..." I look up at my mom then look back down. "Hey

why don't I put my bags away and then I'll play some Nintendo Switch with you two? You wanna play Mario party?"

"Yeah!" they both exclaim simultaneously. My mom gives me a grateful look.

"Only if I get to be Peach!" says Lottie.

"I wanted to be Peach!" says Lola.

"Hey now, I wanted to be Peach," I say, pretending to be offended. "Now go in the living room and behave and I'll meet you there." They both giggle and that gets them to leave the room. I turn and pick up the laundry basket while following my mom upstairs.

"You're so good with them," my mom finally says. "They miss their Uncle Steve. Why the surprise visit?"

"What, I can't come home unannounced?"

"Of course you can, sweetie," says my mom, taking the laundry from me and putting it down. "But don't you have classes?"

"I told my professors I'm going to make up the work tomorrow. It's all independent study art stuff."

"Well that's good. Sounds like you know how your major works. I just want to make sure you're doing well in college." She picks up some little pink shirts and begins to fold them. "You barely tell me about your friends."

"Not too many. To be honest fine art is a solitary practice. But I do go out and get into trouble at bars and stuff. You want me to tell you about that?" I smirk at her for good measure.

"You better not get into too much trouble," my mom replies.

I almost want to add, *"I promise I won't get knocked up as a teenager like my sister,"* but that would be too rude, especially considering Shannon isn't in the room to defend herself or get mad at me. We've all been nothing but supportive since she got pregnant, but as the middle child, it is my duty to give her shit for it.

"I better go downstairs before the girls strangle each other."

"Yes, please, and thank you for helping me babysit. Your sister and your father will be home at 7 maybe."

"Should I order a rotisserie chicken family meal for all of us for dinner?"

"I'll do it later," replies my mom. "Go play with your nieces."

—

After playing Mario Party and watching cartoons, the girls take a nap, and frankly, I'm tempted to join them. They have that five-year-old energy that I'm not used to when I'm at school; I love them but it's exhausting. Eventually my brother Sylvester (everyone calls him "Sly") comes home from his job. He works at a supermarket and is paying his way through his second year of community college. After a brief greeting, he goes into the room that we share to do homework almost immediately. While my hair dangles perfectly, his is slicked back, and ever since I was senior and he was a junior in high school, he's begun to look a lot like me. It's a fact we try not to highlight, as we don't have much in common.

During dinner, my sister and my dad both come home. Since they both were working in the hospital, we all know they have to get out of their scrubs to shower before the girls or myself can hug them. Our meal is a perfectly pleasant time, with delivery being the meal of choice for when we're all home. Between my mom's freelance editing and full-time twin duty, and my brother's after school job, the O'Rourke household doesn't have that many home-cooked meals.

After dinner I insist on playing a board game with the twins (to make sure they don't start any wars) before Shannon helps them get ready for bed at 8.

I haven't been home for more than a week since June since I decided to take some summer art education courses. Being at home is as noisy and cramped as ever, and everyone's so busy that no one seems to relax. My brother barely gave me any snarky remarks, so I can tell how hectic it's been.

Afterwards, I put away the leftovers, clean the dishes, and chat a little with my dad. He asks me the basics *("Do you have enough money? Have you checked the oil on your car?")* before he decides to head to bed. With everyone out of the kitchen, I look out at the darkness of the backyard.

Being home feels comforting, but it reminds me of the reasons why I needed to go to Korham U in the first place: it's too noisy for me here, there's so little space, and the memories of my past relationship haunt me.

I walk out to the backyard and sit at our wooden picnic table. I recall sitting here with Sean simply talking about nothing at all. We were two gay seventeen-year-olds against the world. It felt good to have a boyfriend in high school, someone to call my own. Despite the fights and the inevitable heartbreak, with Sean I never had to hide.

Naturally, my thoughts drift to Ravi. I came here this morning because I needed a breather. Ravi told me to take my time to make a decision, but being away from school hadn't made things clearer. He's sweet, he's gorgeous, but do I really want to date someone in the closet? I did that back in high school, and I don't think I could go through that again.

"Are you okay?" I turn and see Sly walking up to me. "You look, like, really sad." It's dark and he's got his glasses on, so I can't see his eyes. Sometimes I think he wears them when I'm around to make it clear the distinction between the two of us.

"I'm just... I got a lot on my mind. What are you doing out here?"

"I'm come out here sometimes to think."

"No shit. I used to do that all time!"

"Yeah well, I also use this table to study when the twins are being really loud." He sits down across from me diagonally, like he doesn't really want to be seen talking to me. "I'll listen to anything other than kids' cartoons or nursery rhymes, even if it means talking to you."

"I'm touched," I reply, dryly. I can see him smirk in the darkness. A heavy silence passes between us.

"Troubles at university, or with girls? Shit, I mean boys." He shakes his head. "I'm used to asking my guy friends."

"It's cool," I chuckle. I take a deep breath. "There actually is someone."

"Okay."

"He's... well the problem is he's closeted."

"Ah."

"And I'm not."

"Duh."

"And he's captain of the freaking soccer team."

"Woah."

"Yeah, woah," I reply, sarcastically. "Look you're not gonna tell mom or dad about this, right?"

"I don't talk about anyone's romance life, including mine."

"Good," I reply, aggressively.

After a moment of silence, Sly continues, "Well, do you like him?"

I take another deep breath. "Yeah I think I do."

"Does he respect you? Treat you right?"

"I'd say so."

"Well, if you both like each other…" He pauses. "I don't know. It sounds like you two could work through whatever."

"Hmm."

Sly gets up. "I think the real question is 'how are you going to feel if you never give this a shot?' " After a moment he walks across the lawn. "The twins are finally asleep, so, I gotta go get ready for bed. Classes in the morning and all that shit."

"Night bro," I reply. "And stop being so grown-up and wise!" I shout after him. "Pretty soon people will say you're smarter than me!"

"That ship has sailed older brother!" He chuckles as he walks into the house.

My younger brother (who's now way too wise for my liking) has given me a lot to think about. I take out my phone and look at Ravi's name on the screen. I see a few missed texts from an hour ago.

Ravi: *"Simone told me u went home for the day. Hope you're well."*

Ravi: *"Art class wasn't the same without you. (sad face emoji)"*

I smile at the thought of Ravi being concerned about my well-being. I can tell it took him a lot of courage just to reach out, as he's not really one to talk about his feelings. Maybe his little nude-model-strip-tease was really his way of telling me he's interested in me, romantically or sexually (or both).

When I reflect on our time getting to know each other, I find that he hasn't given me any indication that he doesn't respect me, or wouldn't treat me right if we dated. Far from it; when he looks at me, I feel like the coolest guy in the world.

His eyes make me feel like I'm extraordinary, and talking to him puts me at ease. I don't know what he sees in me, but I never want that feeling to go away. I think I know what I have to do.

Sly is right- I don't think I can walk away from this.

13: Ravi

Steven: *"Home was good. I missed my nieces."*

Steven: *"Hopefully art class wasn't so bad. See u Wednesday?"*

Ravi: *"Actually I have an away game. Irons knows about it and I'll make up the work later."*

Ravi: *"Practices are swamping me this week. Maybe Friday we can hang? Get some drawing done?"*

Steven: *"Deal. I'll talk to you later (smiley face emoji)"*

I got those texts late Monday night, and I've been dwelling on them for the past 48 hours. When I was in art class, it scared me noticing that Steven was absent. I began to jump to conclusions: did I freak him out? I asked Simone after class, and she simply said he went back home for the day. I immediately assumed this was my doing. I asked him to take some time to think over the prospect of a date, but I didn't expect him to skip town! I knew I shouldn't have done the nude-model-strip-tease. I bet he thinks I'm messing with him, or that I'm a fuckboy or something.

It's now Wednesday and I still feel like an idiot. Not being able to go to art class today is giving me even more anxiety. Couple that with this away game where I'm supposed to be a good influence on the freshmen, and there's a lot on my plate. If I can't have the guy I like, at least I still have my friends and soccer, two things I know I have a hang on.

--

Tonight, I do not have a hang on things. The away game is disaster. We lose 3 to 0, and I can't help but feel guilty. As co-captain, a lot rests on my shoulders, but tonight's game was especially off for me. I let the other team steal directly from under me twice. My only consolation was noticing that the freshmen, who up until now were coming into their own, were messing up too. We thought they were finally meshing and understanding how us veterans moved and strategized, but tonight it's like we're playing together for the first time.

The next day, with the aura of defeat still lingering, head Coach Dacks pulls me to the side at the beginning of practice.

"Ravi, you know I trust you," he says sternly. With everything happening, I'm already in a sour mood, and the start of Coach's speech is even more unsettling. "You're a good kid, and a good player. You always listen to me."

"Um, thanks?" I just want to go back on the field with the others. I can feel them all looking at us as they run drills.

"Last night's away game was, well, a shit-show," he states bluntly. "But it wasn't just you or Kareem or Landon. It was a team effort, and you know the new guys on the team aren't gelling."

"They've been good other than last night." I attempt to ease the sting of his words. I don't want any new guys to get in trouble.

"Either way, I've come up with a new plan. I want you to take some time today to work on synergizing with one of the freshman."

"What do you mean?"

"Do calisthenics with him, just the two of you. Then go online and watch some of your older games. Then afterward, I don't know." He runs his fingers through his gray hair, then waves his hand in front of his face looking up. "Take him out for a snack, a salad, and talk about girls or something."

"You want us to hang out and be friends?" I ask incredulously.

"I want you to be BEST friends ideally." He says this matter-of-factly, like it's that easy. "This will help bridge the divide that's so obvious on the field between you older guys and the new guys. Plus, it can show him that maybe he can be captain material down the line."

I don't even get a chance to reply when Coach looks away and raises his hand, beckoning someone to come join. I turn to my left to see Paul jogging up to us. He looks guilty but not surprised.

"Coach... captain Ravi." He nods at me.

"Get in there you two." Coach points his thumb backwards.

"Yes coach," we both reply in unison as we walk away from the rest of the team. This is just what my anxiety needed: a forced friendship with some frosh who doesn't want to hang out with me either.

--

We walk down the corridor of the athletics gym to the weight room reserved for team. Logan, the athletics center facilities manager, greets us and takes out his keys to unlock the door.

"Ravi!" he greets, cheerfully. He can't be more than ten-years older than us, and his knowledge of sports and weight-training is top notch. Virtually every athlete gets along with him and we often come to him for wisdom or just to chat. Maybe I should be asking him for help with my boy troubles? "And um... are you Paul?"

"Paul Batalan, Mr. Micucci, sir."

"Woah, woah, Mr. Micucci was my Dad," he chuckles. "It's Logan. Just you two tonight?"

"Yup," I reply, unenthusiastically.

"Oof sorry, I asked." He opens the door and turns on the lights. The weight room illuminates, revealing the familiar sight of rows of elliptical machines, treadmills, and various resistance-training machines. "Look, your away game was just one loss. You'll make up for it in the rest of the season."

"Coach told you about that?" I wince.

"Man, it was so rough the aliens on the moon heard it was bad." Now Paul and I were both wincing at each other. "Okay, that might have been too harsh. I make it a point to stream every game and be up-to-date with most sports teams. I don't just get paid to pick up dirty towels all day. I like to keep an eye on this school's players. Just remember, every game is a chance for you to be a better team."

I smile at this. Logan always seems to know what to say.

"Speaking of streaming, Coach wanted me to review some videos from last season with Paul?"

"Say no more, I'll get the laptop." He leaves and I walk up to an exercise machine. Paul follows me closely, and it irritates me for a moment, before I remember why I'm here.

"Okay, so for calisthenics, people like to ignore their back, but I believe in training every part of my body." I take the large steel bar from above in both hands. As I pull it down, I begin to explain to Paul my process.

--

Two hours later, Paul and I are sitting outside the late night dining hall drinking smoothies and sharing mozzarella sticks and French fries (Coach can go screw himself, I'm not sharing a salad after the week I've had). Talking to Paul is pretty easy now. After working out for an hour and watching my older videos for 45 minutes, I feel him getting more comfortable with me. He still treats me like authority, but at least now he's opening up. I hate to admit it, but it feels like we're becoming friends.

"Don't expect much communication from Landon. The upperclassmen really didn't like him last year," I laugh.

"How am I supposed to understand his body language on the field?" Paul smiles and eats a mozzarella stick.

"I'll work on him," I reply. "He's a stubborn one." We both laugh at this.

I take another long sip of my peanut-butter-kale smoothie. I'm reminded of when I was here two weeks ago or so. Right now it would be very convenient for the rest of the team to interrupt us, so of course, we're left alone.

I'm once again pulled back into the thoughts of Steven. I quickly reach into my pocket to check my phone for new texts, only to find no notifications.

"Is something the matter?" asks Paul. His eyes look genuinely concerned.

"Uh no."

Paul looks down at the table. "When coach told me to meet up with you, he told me to talk to you about girls or some shit." He giggles at this. "Like that's gonna make us better on the field or something."

I look down at my food as well. It would feel really good to be able to talk about shit with someone, anyone. I can't keep going to Simone for advice, she's best friends with Steven. This freshman has been acting like I'm royalty since summer training. Aw fuck it.

"Actually there is... someone... I could use some advice on."

"Really?" he asks, way too eager.

"Slow it down Gossip Girl." I put my hand up. "It's not that interesting."

"Understood sir, uh, Ravi," he corrects himself. "So, what's going on with this... person?"

I notice his distinct lack of gendered pronouns.

"I may have... come on to this... person kinda strong." I look down at the table, playing with a French fry aimlessly.

I pause for a moment, take a deep breath and continue. "To top it off, people on the team might not... respect me as much if I'm dating this person. I'm afraid the team won't accept me if they find out." I look away. "I've never, like, actually dated anyone before. But what I want more than anything..."

"You want to be with this person," states Paul, finishing my sentence.

"Yeah." There's a moment of silence. All we can hear is the buzzing of the machines in the dining hall several yards away.

"My dad always tells me to follow my heart. If you do, it'll be hard to regret what happens after."

I look up at Paul. He's a baby-faced kid, but his eyes seem perpetually genuine.

"I say go for it. If your friends don't accept that, then screw them."

"I don't know if I can say that to the whole team, or to Coach Dacks."

"Pssh. Fuck that. I'm on the team. And I know the other new guys look up to you. We may only be freshmen, but we got your back." He smiles at me.

"Thanks."

Paul looks down at his phone. "Shit, I gotta go, it's getting late and I have class at 8 in the morning tomorrow."

"Damn, sorry man," I say, standing up.

"No worries. This was fun. And don't worry your secret's safe with me." He smiles at me while he throws away his plate.

"What secret?"

"This person you like?" He looks around to make sure no one is eavesdropping. "It's not a girl, is it?" He shrugs.

Have I really been so transparent? I kind of stare at him, unable to respond.

"You don't have to reply," he says quickly. "I didn't hear a thing. I'll see you at practice tomorrow!" With a wave, he walks away.

I guess that's one way to come out to a friend.

14: Steven

Not seeing Ravi in art class on Wednesday was torture. Not being able to resolve any of this in person is also torture, and I'm acutely aware that this is partially my doing.

It's Friday morning and Ravi and I have barely gotten to text since his away game Wednesday. Apparently they lost miserably and now they're doing team bonding for damage control (whatever that means). Today I'm in a downstairs studio, meeting with my fine arts major advisor, Prof. Garcia. She's an older woman about the same age as Deirdre, but she's not nearly as loud. She's quiet but commands respect in the room, making her the perfect mentor to keep me in line.

I watch her thumbing through my portfolio, nodding silently with her glasses on. While she does, my thoughts drift on how to approach Ravi the right way, all while making sure his intentions are genuine.

"You've managed to catch up on the coursework, Steven. Glad to see all the independent studying in DI101 is worth it."

"Yes well Prof. Irons has always been a real help."

"These models that you've gotten are impressive. I've always thought you should expand your subject matter beyond the smaller nature details you love so much."

"I do love a good mushroom," I add, trying not to take offense. "The human body has plenty to offer too." Oh great, now I'm thinking about Ravi's human body, so sculpted and strong- no, I need to concentrate.

"I know it's not your favorite, but a diverse portfolio is what you need for any fine arts degrees. I'm glad you're exploring other subject matters."

"Thanks."

"Are you thinking about developing any of these into a print? I know you know how to use the inking station."

"Well..." I trail off. I hadn't thought of it, but an idea begins to form. "Can I use it today? If Prof. Irons says it's okay? I'd love to develop one of these model figures into something bigger."

"I'm sure that can be arranged. I'll call her." She hands back my portfolio with a smile.

For the first time in weeks I feel like I'm in control and I know what to do. I need to get to work though, there's a lot to be done.

—

Later that night, well after soccer practice is over, I push the dial button on my phone. To my flattery, Ravi answers on the second ring.

"Hello?"

"Hey Ravi! Glad I caught you."

"Hey! Uh… let me just step into my room where it's quiet." After a moment I hear a door close. "What's up Steven?"

"I missed you in art class on Wednesday."

"Yeah well I keep missing you. That last time we worked together was…" Thoughts of the day that Ravi took off his clothes in front of me come to mind. "I don't know when."

"Right." I smile.

"How was home?"

"Home was good. It gave me plenty of time to… reexamine things."

"Oh," he replies, with a careful sound of neutrality. "So how are you feeling now?"

"Well that depends. Are you busy right now?"

"Uh, no, not really."

"Then I have a surprise for you. Get your jacket, let's take a walk."

"Right now?"

"If you're free."

"Yeah, yeah I am. Where are you?"

"I'm… at the spot where you hugged me for the first time. Do you remember that night?"

"I did what? Oh… oh yeah." He chuckles. "I was an idiot."

"Meet me there, BUT only if you promise to walk with me and NOT to talk until we get to our destination. Deal?"

"Deal. Wait, you're in front of my building?"

"Tick tock Ravi." I immediately hang up before he gets any more confused.

I stare up at the athlete's dorm. The front of it has massive windows, so at night, you can see who's wandering the halls. Not even a minute later, I see Ravi walk up to the window.

He puts his face to the glass and covers his eyes so he can see me through the darkness outside. I smile and wave, and I see him smile back. He waves and runs down to the staircase. Could he be any more adorable?

After he bursts through the doors, I nod my head and power-walk away with him trailing me.

"It's really good to see you," he says, out of breath (I'm not sure why he's winded).

"Likewise," I reply, refusing to look him in the eye. I'm borderline sprinting now, down across the quad.

After a beat, Ravi says, "Where are we going?"

"No talking." I smirk at him. "Just trust me."

He smiles and nods.

We finally make it to the fine arts building. It's pretty late on a Friday, so no one is around.

"Are we going to the studio?" I just stare at him with a wicked grin. He continues, "Look about last week, you don't have to respond or anything. I was just being stupid. If you don't wanna date, I'm cool with that too. I'll just ignore my feelings and, and, and-"

"Ravi, I mean this in the kindest way: shut up." I smile at him and open the next set of double doors. I lead him around a corner, and point.

"What is this?" he asks, breathless as ever. His eyes fill with wonder as he gazes on the wall.

The fine arts building has large walled areas where students can showcase their works intermittently. Today, I took the liberty of hanging up my latest print. I spent three hours making two different types of ink and re-doing a large version of Ravi's almost-nude body sketch. I added splashes of black shapes across his face and crotch area so that he couldn't be identified. The final result showcased his abs, arms, and thighs with blasts of orange around him, like some sort of angelic silhouette.

"I uhh..." I dig my sneaker in the floor. "I did this today. Um, surprise?" Ravi continues to stare at my work, mouth wide open. "I hope you like it?" I ask, my voice much quieter. I hadn't realized my hands were shaking.

"You... you... What? How?"

"I got to do some printmaking today. I made multiple inks. It's barely dry, and um, I'm actually not even supposed to hang it up here, since it's not my turn to use this space, but I thought *'hey, why not?'* so I grabbed some tacks and uh, voila!" I wave my hands at my piece to stop myself from babbling even more.

"That's me?" he asks incredulously, still not looking at me.

"Yeah." I smile, knowing that my face is full on red at this point. I'd never been nervous to share work before. What is this boy doing to me? "Do you like it?" My voice is barely a whisper.

With that, Ravi turns to look at me. He says nothing, but his eyes are reaching for me, telling me things he can't say. "It's... You're so talented!" He's still not looking at my work, but directly into my eyes. "I can't believe you did this. Steven, you're amazing."

That's it. That's all Ravi needed to say to get me to like him more than I already did. I touch his shoulder and lead him to a corner, where there aren't a hundred studio lights and a massive window to the courtyard; from here, no one can see us. In the darkness, I can still see him staring at me.

"Ravi, I've given it a lot of thought, but... I'm done overthinking things. If your offer still stands, I'd like to give this a shot. Us." I point at both of us. "Dating. 'Cause... I like you." I reach out and take his hand in mine.

I can see him smiling but he's still not talking. He threads his fingers into mine and I pull him closer. His face is so close to mine, I swear I can hear his heart beating. I feel his body heat emanating onto me. Not wanting to waste the moment or get interrupted, I put my hand other hand on his cheek. I caress his stubble, causing him to close his eyes. I pull him closer and finally put his lips on mine.

15: Ravi

I've kissed a few girls back in high school, but it was *NOTHING* like this. Kissing someone you actually like (someone you *really* like) is phenomenal. It's incredible. It's a paradise between the two of us. It's fireworks. It's a burning red supernova, and I want it to last forever. Kissing Steven is all that and more.

After a moment he pulls back and I take a breath. I finally open my eyes to get a good look at him. Even in the dark, he's beautiful, and I can tell he's trying to appraise if it felt right to me. My breath becomes ragged, and I respond by taking the back of his head and kissing him again. Only this time, there is no hesitancy, only passion. I part his lips and flick my tongue across his, and I swear my eyes roll back.

Some say kissing is an art, and Steven is literally the most talented artist I've ever known.

After a few more moments of basically making out, I let out a moan and pull back. I'm getting way too excited here, and I'm not about to blow this moment by, well, blowing my load in my pants. Though, if we keep this up, I doubt I'd care who was around or where we were. With Steven kissing me, nothing else in the universe seems to exist.

I stroke his cheek one more time and he smiles at me. "You're incredible," I whisper.

"Right back ya, soccer captain." He grins. After another moment of stroking his gorgeous face, he closes his eyes. "We should probably get going."

"Yeah," I agree reluctantly. "One more for the road?" I grin at him and he returns it by kissing me on the cheek. I swear that will never get old.

"That's all for now." He walks me out back into the illuminated corridor, back into the real world. "Besides, you play your cards right, there's much more where that came from." His mischievous grin and his innuendo-laden tone make my insides flutter. "As I recall, you said you wanted to take me on a date."

"Uhh…" I shake my head to snap out of it. "Right. Right!" I nod as we walk side-by-side through the hallways. We're not touching anymore, which sucks, but the energy between has changed. "Tomorrow night?"

"Sounds good," he chuckles. We walk out of the fine arts building and awkwardly pause and look at each other. "Well, I guess I better go back to my dorm." He points his thumb the opposite direction of my place.

"You want me to walk you?"

"Save it for the first date, stud. You'll get to see my place soon enough." Even in the darkness I can see him wink at me. I swear, I might never stop grinning. He turns his heel and says, "Good night Ravi."

"Night!" I shout back. As I walk back to my dorm through

the night, I pump my fist through the air just once to celebrate tonight, but only with myself.

--

I return to see my suitemates all watching a movie.

"Where did you run off to?" asks Landon, grabbing a fistful of popcorn.

"I had to... um..." I look down. Shit, what should I say? "I had to call my mom. And you fuckers are too noisy."

"Hey, when Batman starts punching Superman, we gotta crank the volume."

"Right." I'm about to ditch them to go back into my room when it dawns on me: I'm going on a date tomorrow, but I have no idea what that entails! What do two guys do on first dates? What does Steven like? How can I impress him?

I turn around to see Omar eating popcorn next to Landon who's on the couch next to Kareem. I recall him more-or-less admitting he's bisexual. He must know a thing or two about dating the same sex, right? I awkwardly walk back into the living area and try to calm my nerves.

"Hey Omar, can I like, talk to you when you're free?" The boys all turn their heads and look at me as if I started speaking an alien language. Then Landon and Kareem turn to Omar, just as confused.

"Uhh..." Omar looks at them, then back up at me. "Sure." He puts the popcorn on Kareem's lap and follows me into my room.

My single room is the one modicum of privacy that I never let anyone into. The walls are moderately thick but I try not to talk too loudly anyway. Omar sits down at my desk while stand near my bed.

"So..." I begin, putting my hands together in front of my face, like I'm praying.

97

"So."

"Look this is weird, but I kind of have a date tomorrow."

"Ooh *la la*," Omar sings at me.

"And I don't know what to do."

"What do you mean?"

"I mean I've never actually taken anyone on a real date before."

"Seriously? Not even in high school?"

"It was always, like double dates, or prom and shit. And I never really cared about those girls."

"Okay, well, not that I mind, but why are you asking me? I don't really do dates. I'm kind of a fuckboy. Kareem is the one who has a new girlfriend every semester."

"Yeah but they um…" How do I put this correctly? "They date girls, and that dynamic is different. You're the only one I know who's dated or hooked up with…" I trail off hoping he understands.

"Hooked up with… oh." His eyes are blown wide now with realization. "OH!" I nod sheepishly. "Okay okay." He looks down and nods. "Okay this explains a lot. UMM, alright."

"Yeah," I reply.

"Okay, so you're going on a date with… you know what? Don't tell me who it is. My point is that you've got a date? Like for real?"

"Yup. I asked this PERSON out," I say, emphasizing a lack of pronouns.

"Well why don't you take them to something that they like?" He turns and opens up the laptop at my desk. "We'll use the power of the internet to search your date's interests!" I lean over and type my password in and open a browser.

"Alright. Let's do a search for…" Omar trails off and looks

up. "Art galleries or museums?" He looks at me with a knowing grin and I stare back at him in horror. "Just a shot in the dark buddy! No need to be alarmed."

He types it in and there happen to be some gallery openings tomorrow within five miles. Score.

"Alright, but I don't have a car."

"You can borrow my car." He stands up proudly. "As long as you promise me one thing." He puts his hands on my shoulders and looks me in the eye dramatically. "Don't have sex in my car."

Omar's barely containing a giggle while I stare at him with fury and push his hands off. I'm so flustered all I can do is open my door. He walks out laughing and leaves to his own room. As he does, Landon walks by my doorway with a concerned expression.

"Is everything okay Ravi?"

"Just peachy," I mutter standing by my door, ready to close it. Just then, Omar comes out of his room and walks up to me and Landon.

"Oh, and by the way..." He grabs my hand and proceeds to put a chain of about six condoms right into my palm. "You're welcome." He's beaming at me. As he giggles away, Landon and I look down with a mixture of shock and embarrassment.

Sometimes I hate my friends.

16: Steven

I hate to admit it, but I'm nervous as fuck. It's not just because I like Ravi (I do), but it's because I haven't been on a first date since high school. I unbutton the collar on my shirt; it's too revealing. I button it up again, but now I can't breathe. Ravi told me to dress nicely and that he'd be picking me up, but he wouldn't provide any other details, and I'm not one for surprises.

He texts me that he's in front of my dorm, and I bolt out of my room. As I walk down the pathway, I nervously breathe in the cold autumn air. I see Ravi in a dark brown compact car and he waves at me. I smile back as I approach him. Maybe it's 'first date' nerves, but seeing him leaves me breathless.

"Hey!" I step into the passenger seat and fumble with the seatbelt.

"Hey man," he replies as he shifts the gear. He pulls away

and begins to drive off campus. I turn to my left to get a good look at him. He's got a dark blue button-down shirt on over black slacks and a black blazer. How can he look like a model in literally every outfit?

"You look good." I smile at him, hoping I don't sound as anxious as I am.

"Uh thanks. You do too." He side-eyes me. "You look very good."

"Alright, enough pleasantries." I giggle. "Where are you taking me?"

"Just trust me. Isn't that what you always say?"

"Ha ha, okay, I deserve that." I put my hands up in defeat.

We spend the next five minutes chatting about nothing in particular while he weaves down the highway. I ask about his classes and he asks about how my visit home was. Eventually we make it to a downtown residential area and pull up to what looks like an old mansion.

"Are we going to the Barrett Center?"

"Yeah, if that's cool?" he asks, biting his lip. He's adorable.

"Yeah, I didn't think people knew about it."

"Hey, dumb jocks like me can still use the internet." He smiles. "There's an exhibit opening tonight." He pulls into a parking space on the gravel, where seven other cars are parked. "Thought it might be fun."

I'm touched that he took the time to research something like this. "Alright. Let's go!"

I hastily open my door and I catch him running around to my side of the car. "Sorry," he says, out-of-breath. "I was trying to open your door for you, like a gentleman."

Sheesh, he is a nervous wreck. "No need," I smile, looking into his eyes. "You don't have to treat me like royalty or something. Let's just act like we're two friends."

101

"Friends?" he asks, concerned.

"Friends who HAPPEN to be on a date," I quickly correct. "Romantically." With that I take his hand and he gives me a quick smile before we walk up the steps.

We split up as Ravi goes to pay the entrance fee. The Barrett Center is this old mansion that was converted in the 70's into a make-shift museum on the inside. I had been there before for some art extra credit excursions. Immediately upon entering, you are greeted with three hallways, each a large sweeping corridor that houses artwork and connect in the back. There's a table in the foyer with some complimentary crackers, cheese, and beverages. After Ravi finishes paying, we decide to walk down the left where a few other people are already roaming about.

"Have you been to one of these before?"

"No," he admits, sounding defeated.

"They're pretty cool, usually," I reply trying to lift his spirits. I look around to see that this month's exhibit is on urban photography. Truthfully, it's not a point of interest for me, but Ravi doesn't need to know that.

After some time walking down the winding corridor, occasionally pausing at photographs, I decide to continue some small talk.

"I didn't know you had a car."

"I don't. I'm borrowing one of my suitemate's cars. You remember Omar?"

"Oh yeah, the guy who said I was good-looking," I muse.

"I thought you were good-looking first," mutters Ravi, looking away.

"That's awesome that he let you borrow his car." Ravi turns to look at me. "It means a lot that you took the time to arrange that."

"Yeah, well, I didn't wanna take the bus," he says, scratching the back of his head.

"Look I have a car. For our next date, let me take us somewhere." Ravi stops walking and I'm forced to stop and turn around.

"Next date?" I look back to see Ravi beaming. I smile and reach to take his hand.

"This date isn't over yet, but so far, I'd say you're passing the bar." I lace his fingers into mine, and just like the first time I did, I feel the sparks.

--

We spend the rest of our time chatting about everything and nothing at all. I'm legitimately having a good time because, as always, being with Ravi feels easy. He's gentle and actually listens to me when I talk. He asks about what kind of art I'm working on, and in turn, I ask him how the season is going. We discuss the artwork on the wall for a bit, and I can tell he's trying really hard to be into it.

After about 30 minutes of strolling around, we make it back to the entrance way and start walking the circle again. I'm getting bored of urban landscape black-and-white photos, so I can tell this must be torture for Ravi. I've got my hands in my jacket pocket and I see him pick up another free cracker with cheese.

"Do you wanna do another lap?" he asks, inhaling his food.

"Nah, I think I'm good. Photography isn't really my favorite." A slight panic flashes on his face. "I'm having an awesome time though! With you, it's always a good time." I bump my elbow into his as he smiles with relief.

"We could um, get food?"

"When was the last time you ate something other than crackers? I thought you jocks need to eat a meal every two hours or you'll die."

"I kinda skipped dinner?" he replies, sheepishly. "I was too busy shopping."

"Did you buy clothes just for tonight?"

"Um…" He shrugs, making it very clear. "Maybe? I've never been to a gallery opening, so I wasn't sure what to wear."

I'm touched. "That's really sweet of you."

"Do you wanna go back to campus?"

I look at my phone to check the time. "It's still pretty early. I'm not ready for this date to be over yet."

"Me neither," he beams. "But I didn't have any other plans in mind."

An idea pops into my head. "Why don't we get out of here? I'd like to take you somewhere a bit more…" I look around. No one is within earshot. "Busy?"

"Um," he replies, puzzled.

"There's plenty of food there."

"Sold."

--

Five minutes later, I manage to convince Ravi to let me drive. We once again hit the highway, but only for a bit before we're back on local roads. Ten minutes later, we pull up to a separate downtown area with several bars. After I park, I lead him to my destination of choice. His eyes light up at the sign.

"The Player One Bar?"

"Yeah, come on in." I hold open the door for him. We walk in together and take a seat by the bar.

The Player One Bar is partly a traditional bar with food and partly an arcade with games in the back. As such, it's fairly noisy, but I've never had a problem having a conversation here. Patrons are encouraged to buy beer, eat, and play games.

"I've been here a few times. It's a hidden gem in town." We take a seat at a booth.

"This place is awesome!" He smiles at me.

"You're just saying that because the menu has more than crackers and grapes," I retort, lifting up the menu.

"Doesn't mean it's not awesome." We both laugh.

"Alright, order what you want, 'cause after we eat, I'm kicking your ass at foosball."

"Oh really?" he asks, with a challenging grin on his face. "You think you can beat a varsity soccer player at foosball?"

"You might be the star on the turf, but little plastic arcade prongs? That's MY territory!"

"You're on, O'Rourke." He laughs. "Wanna make it interesting?"

I look up and tap my chin. "Hmm... okay." I stare him down, confidently. "Winner gets to pick what we do after this, to finish off the date."

He looks puzzled. "Deal, but what did you have in mind?"

"Well my roommate's away for the night." I take Ravi's hand in mine across the table and stroke my thumb across his hand slowly. I look him in the eyes and say, "If I win, I'm taking you home."

17: Ravi

I don't think I've ever driven back to campus and parked that quickly before. Back at The Player One Bar, we ate delicious burgers and fries. I may have deliberately not eaten as much I wanted, a side effect of nerves and knowing that a full stomach does NOT help in sexy situations. I had to act like I was interested in other arcade games and tried my best to casually lose at foosball. Steven could totally tell I was holding back, but honestly, he's a pretty good foosball player.

Regardless, he won, and now here we are, in front of his dorm, our faces illuminated only by the lights in the building. He looks at me, blushing and smiling. This has a fluttering effect on my body, and I was already buzzing with nervousness and (horny) anticipation.

"I had a really good time tonight Ravi," he says, hands in his pockets.

"I did too, but it's not over, right?"

"I did beat you at foosball." He shrugs and looks off to the side.

"And a deal's a deal." I smile at him.

"Look," he says, closing his eyes. "I don't wanna do anything you're not comfortable with."

"I'm comfortable with it!" I blurt, almost too quickly.

"I don't want to push you too far. I want to respect your... your boundaries, 'cause, I like you, and... and..." he stammers.

Holy shit. He's actually concerned that he's taking advantage of me or something.

"Steven." He finally looks at me. I lean into his ear, and whisper with my huskiest voice, "Take me to your room, and I'll show you exactly where my boundaries are."

His eyebrows jump and he immediately whips out his ID card to open up the door.

—

We finally make it up to his room and he unlocks the door. I look left and right to see if anyone is spying on us before I enter. It's small and lived in, and the two beds are way too close for my liking. Still, it feels so comfortable; maybe it's because of the familiar artwork hanging on his side of the room, or maybe because its smells so much like Steven. Regardless, I can see myself spending a lot of time here. I look out the window and only see trees shrouded in darkness.

I hear the door close behind me and turn around to see Steven leaning against it. His expression is decidedly neutral as he looks down. I get closer to him to ask him what the problem is, but I'm immediately assaulted by him grabbing my jacket collar, pulling me in, and putting his lips on mine.

I don't know if anything will ever top that first kiss we had, but this is a damn strong contender. Gone is the tenuousness from before. Now, his lips are aggressive, his tongue is dominant, and his moans are drenched with lust. He tastes amazing and I never want him to stop.

I've learned over a dozen things about Steven tonight, but his horny kissing technique is my favorite.

I decide to return the favor by pressing him against the door, my left hand leaning on it by the side of his shoulder. It's like I've trapped him here, but he's the one who pulled me in- so really, who is taking advantage of whom?

"Fuck Ravi..." he pleads, moaning breathlessly between kisses. "Bed- mm- now." He points to his left, and I immediately listen to his orders, first taking off my jacket. Before I get a chance to get to my shirt, I turn to see him staring at me, lips still red from all the making out we just did.

"We should-" he says, still breathing rapidly. "Um, we should probably talk about those boundaries now."

"Right." I nod in response.

"Because if you get on that bed, there's no way I'm pulling the brakes." He sounds breathless and serious, but I nod still. "So tell me what you wanna do Ravi, and I'll do it. Probably." He smiles.

My heart pounds in anticipation. "Uh... what do you wanna do?"

He grins at me and begins unbuttoning his shirt. Now, it's his turn to lean in and whisper. "I want my mouth on every part of you, including your cock." Is it possible to freeze and boil over at the same time? Because I just shivered and got hard instantly. I nod at him.

"Are you sure?" he asks, ripping off his shirt. He's wearing a tight white tank top underneath. Fuck how am I supposed to speak words when he looks like that?

"So, so sure." I grab his left arm and start kissing up and down his bicep. "This is hot."

"You like that?"

"Fuck yeah. Been wanting this ever since you were making ink in class." I start to place kisses near his underarm, then trail them up to his well-defined deltoid, then onto his clavicle. "I saw your arms for the first time. It was so fucking hot." I moan against his skin. It's true; while I've seen dozens of athletic guys in the locker rooms over the years, none of them got me going as much as Steven.

"I may have been flexing to impress you," he admits, moaning and closing his eyes tightly.

I look up at him. "Consider me impressed." I grab the back of his head and kiss him some more before pulling away. I start to unbutton my shirt, when he bats my hands away.

"Please, allow me." He grins wickedly at me and begins to slowly unbutton me. He's barely touching me, I'm wearing clothes, and this may be the sexiest moment of my life (no it DEFINITELY is).

"Ravi... why did you model for me that day?" he asks, his voice deep with lust.

"Because," I barely breathe out, eyes closed. "I wanted you to-"

"You wanted me to stare didn't you?"

"Yes."

He removes another button revealing my chest. "You wanted me turned on," he continues, his breath dancing on my chest. "You wanted me to be so horny for you."

"Yessss," I hiss, as he continues to undress me.

"You wanted me to worship you." He plants a kiss in

between my pecs and pushes away more fabric to the side. My eyes roll back.

"Yes." I'm barely audible at this point.

"Well you have me now." He pulls his tank top off and over his head, all while staring at me. Fuck, who said artists weren't fit? Before I can really enjoy his tight, toned body, he leans forward and takes my nipple into his mouth.

"FUCK!" I cry out. No one's ever done this to me before. How has no one ever done this to me before? I feel like 100 fireworks have gone off in my eyes.

"Shh," he says. "Dorm rooms. Thin walls." Then he proceeds to suck on my other nipple. I put my fist into my mouth and moan. I'm almost in tears it feels so good.

After an ecstasy-filled eternity of this, he pushes me onto the bed. He sinks to his knees and palms my hardness through my pants. I lean back, my whole upper body on display. I raise one hand, running it through his hair, and look at him. He's beautiful, and now, his eyes are filled with so much hunger- I can't believe it's for me.

"May I?" he asks, grabbing my belt.

"Please," I beg.

He undoes my belt and pulls down my pants and boxers in one movement. I should feel self-conscious. I should feel weird that he's a guy. I should be concerned because I'm basically a virgin. I should be freaking out.

Instead, I feel nothing but lustful anticipation. Steven does this to me: he's pushed me past my comfort zone since day one, and I've loved every moment of it.

He takes my hard dick in his hand and looks at it like it's a treasure. Then he licks just the tip, and my eyes roll back again. After a moment, he sinks the whole first half into his mouth and my whole head falls backward. I feel him suck and swallow and lick at all the right places. His mouth is so wet and greedy, like I'm his favorite treat.

Steven O'Rourke is devilishly methodical when it comes to the art of oral sex.

After an embarrassingly short amount of time, I start panting. "I'm gonna-" I say, gripping his hair tighter. He moans in response around my cock. I look down and see his pretty face, lips engulfing me, and that's all it takes.

"FUCK!" I shout again, not even bothering to hide it. I come right then and there, and I'm lost in the stars of orgasmic bliss. For the next 45 seconds, nothing in the universe exists except my soul and Steven's mouth.

After some time of not remembering my own name, I feel Steven crawl into bed next to me. Next, I feel the familiar rhythm of someone jerking off. I open my eyes to see him staring right at me, mouth agape, while he strokes himself off. I reach over and grab his dick. He's rock hard, and it's so warm in my hand. He thrusts into me twice, no three times, then shudders, lips biting back a moan. He comes through my fingers and it thrills me to know that I'm partly responsible. I make a mental note to remember that I want to make him feel that way with my mouth (and maybe even my ass?) someday soon.

--

We lay like that for several more minutes, a sticky entwined mess, with our breathing slowly returning to normal. Eventually, he gets up and grabs an old shirt to clean up both of us. Then, we shuck off the rest of our clothes and lie in bed together, pulling over the blanket.

I trace my hand on his back while he lies with his head on my chest. My eyelids are getting heavy, but I don't want this night to end.

"Was this... a good date?" I whisper.

"I was gonna ask you the same question." I know what he's really asking me. He wants to know how he performed.

"It was the best. Better than I could have ever imagined. You made me feel..." I search for the words. "Feel amazing. So, so good."

I feel him smile against me. "It was the best for me too."

18: Steven

The next morning, Ravi wakes me up at 6 by going to the bathroom, wearing only his pants from last night. After he returns, I don't even need to ask him to stay and cuddle, he just shucks off his pants and crawls right back into bed, naked. I yawn against him and go back to sleep.

Being with Ravi makes me feel content and safe. He makes me feel strong, talented, and admired. This feeling should scare me, and somewhere deep inside it does. I have so many insecurities bubbling up, but I tamp them down and just enjoy sleeping next to him.

I just scored the captain of my college soccer team- talk about winning the 'hot-jock-sex-lottery'!

I eventually wake up again and look at my phone to see it's already 9:30. I look over and see Ravi starting to wake up as well.

"Morning," he mutters with a smile on his face.

"Morning." My anxiety is starting to rise up again. Is he going to act like last night wasn't a big deal? Was this a one-and-done? Has he gotten his "experimentation" out of his system and now he's going back to the safety of heterosexuality?

He strokes my cheek with his thumb. "What's wrong?"

"It's nothing," I reply, rolling over and staring at the ceiling.

"Steven."

"Fine." I let out a long breath and buzz my lips, putting my hands over my face, then pulling them back down. "I guess I have this fear that you're gonna lose interest now."

"What?!"

"I'm afraid now that you've *'gotten it out of your system'* you won't call me back anymore."

"What?!" he exclaims again, confused. "Steven, I-"

"I know it's stupid." I side-eye to look at him. "Just forget it."

"I don't wanna forget it." Hearing this, I turn to study him. How is he still so good-looking the morning after, no shower or anything? "I don't want any secrets between us. I want you to feel good about being... with me."

"How could I not wanna be with you, even before last night?"

"So I earned myself another date then?" His smirk has returned.

"Cuddle with me some more and I'll take it into serious consideration." I throw him a playful stern look. He giggles and moves onto my chest. God, him lying on my heart feels so right. I stroke my hand behind his (chiseled) back for a few more moments.

"Can I ask you something?"

"Always."

"Have you ever had sex with girls?" I feel him freeze up. "It's okay if you have. I never actually asked what you identify as, and everyone has a past."

He pulls off and gives me a serious look.

"Honestly?"

"Please."

"No I haven't."

"Seriously?"

"Seriously. I've been pretty much frigid to all the girls here at KU."

"I saw that first-hand," I chuckle. "What about in high school? Surely some prom date was trying to get in your pants."

"Lots of girls have tried to get in my pants. If we're telling the truth…" He rolls over and stares at the ceiling. "On prom night I did get a little drunk and I… let my date jerk me off. But that was it: an awkward hand job from some girl in high school that neither of us really enjoyed."

"Huh," I reply. "And nothing since then?"

"No one's gotten into my pants unless I wanted them too." The wicked grin returns to his face. "And last night I really, really wanted you to."

I smile at him. "Anything to help the soccer captain."

"How about you?"

"What?"

"Past sexual experiences?"

"All of them?" I ask, surprised.

"Well, how far have you gone?"

"Well," I start, unsure of how honest I should be. "In high

school, I regularly made out with this one guy in secret."

"Yeah?"

"Yeah. He was on the varsity tennis team, so handsome, long legs, the works. We had been flirting for weeks and finally, we hung out at his place after school to do homework and..."

"And one thing led to another?"

"Yup."

"So what happened?"

I take a deep breath as I bring up the painful memory. "After hooking up a few times, he eventually told me point blank that dating girls was just easier, so then he stopped talking to me. Blocked my number and everything. That was rough." I pull off a piece of lint from my bare chest.

"Steven, I would never do that to you."

"I know."

"I'm sorry you went through that." He kisses my shoulder. "He sounds like an ass."

"Yeah well... after that I met Sean. We dated for almost 3 years."

"Right," he replies. "So you two did, um, everything?"

"Yup."

"Okay." He's silent for a moment. "I feel weird, being a virgin and all."

"Except for last night." I wink at him and he smiles.

"I'm just not experienced," he continues. "I... I-I'm aware it's not something you ideally want in a boyfriend."

"Boyfriend?"

He looks panicked at this point. "Um. Eventually. Maybe. If you're cool with it."

I giggle and lean in and kiss him. "How about we go out next weekend, and see where things go from there?"

"Deal," he beams at me. "Guess I earned that second date after all."

I laugh and lay my head on the pillow staring at the ceiling. He gets up and starts to get dressed. He doesn't realize it, but he's very quickly earning a lot more of me than I'd wanted so soon. It should scare me, but just maybe, Ravi will be worth it.

--

Keeping my budding relationship with Ravi a secret is equal parts frustrating and hot. We can barely keep our hands off each other during art class. Simone is mad that I won't give her explicit details about my date, but she keeps making funny faces at us in art class. On top of that, my roommate is always around now, so we can't have in-between class hook-up sessions. Between my projects and his practices, we've barely gotten to see each other at all this week, which also sucks.

Still, it's now Saturday night, and we finally get some time alone. After some light arguing, I convince him to let me drive him on our date, since I have a car. One minute after he gets into the passenger seat, I manage to hit a stop sign and look over at him to see him already staring at me.

Grateful for the stop, I lean over and kiss him. I'm firm, but gentle, because there'll be plenty of time later for making out. "You look real handsome tonight," I remark, finally turning back to the steering wheel.

"Thanks. You do too." I swear I can hear him blushing. After two more minutes on the highway, I hear Ravi ask "I take it you're not gonna tell me where we're going?"

"Now you're getting the hang of it!" I'm full on grinning at him as I drive through the dark.

While I cruise, we catch up on our day, chatting about all the things that went on. His business classes seem involved, but that's nothing compared to what the coach is putting them through. Ravi's life at school is so different than mine, but I enjoy learning about all the little things that make up who he is.

A few minutes later, I pull into the parking lot of our destination. "Cosmic Putt-putt?" he asks.

"Yes sir." I pull into a parking spot. "You got to pick the last place we went to. Now I wanted to take you here."

"Hey, you got to take me to the Player One bar after!"

"And maybe, you can pick where we go AFTER this time." I wink at him as I pull up the parking brake. I swear, making him blush will never get old to me.

We make our way into Cosmic Putt-putt: It's an indoor miniature golf facility, complete with a small snack bar and several arcade games. Since it's October, they've got plenty of orange lights and cobwebs around as décor; it's corny and childish, and I love it.

"Okay, so, pizza or arcade games?" I ask, eagerly as I walk backwards.

"Uhh, didn't you wanna go mini-golfing?"

"I did, but I wanted to eat first or play a game."

"Alright." He nods at me with a semi-serious expression. It dawns on me that maybe this date was too immature.

"Sorry," I cringe. "Is this place lame?" I stop and look around. "We can go somewhere else. There's probably a gallery somewhere."

"It's not lame, it's awesome." He grabs my arms and leans in. "I'll have fun with you no matter what." He looks into my eyes and I feel my heart melt.

"That's exactly why I wanted to take you here, to show you that I don't need fancy galleries for us to be on a date. I just wanna hang out with you, no matter where."

He looks serious again and pulls me in for a tight hug. "Thanks Steven. I want that too." I take a moment to enjoy his warmth.

"I've missed holding you all week," I murmur against his shoulder.

"Well you're not gonna miss it after I beat you at air hockey." He runs up to a nearby table and raises a challenging eyebrow.

"Hey," I laugh. "You're supposed to win me a stuffed animal at one of these games first."

"Pssh, you're just afraid you're gonna lose." We both laugh as I fish out some quarters to start playing the game.

—

We spend the next two hours playing games, eating pizza, and playing one round of mini golf. I'm having an amazing time and it feels like we're the only ones in the building. I swear, the smile hasn't left my face since we got here; Ravi has this power to just make me happy constantly.

"I gotta say, I bet I could make varsity putt putt," I joke as we walk out the door.

"Oh totally. Form a petition and make it happen at KU."

"But only if there are aliens and spaceships on the field."

"Obviously." He smiles as he gets into the passenger seat.

I lift up the stuffed toy that Ravi won me from the arcade claw machine. It's a 6-inch tall fat brown owl with heart eyes. "Here ya go little buddy," I coo, placing him on my dashboard.

"Aww, he has a nest now," Ravi adds.

"Exactly," I laugh. Before I start the car, I turn to look at him. There's a weighted silence, and the tension between us ramps as we stare at each other. It's dark, and I stare at his face illuminated by the glow of the outside street lamp. I want to make a move, but a question is holding me back.

"Before we do anything, can I ask you something?"

"Of course."

"Are you going to tell your teammates about us?"

"I uh, already sort of told Omar. He's bi, I think."

"Okay... and the others?"

Ravi looks down for a moment. After what feels like forever he whispers, "I want to. I swear I will."

"Okay," I reply. I knew that going into this. "I can wait." A part of me is saying *"He already told one person, so that's a start right?"* A bigger part of me is telling me to back out now. It won't break my heart as much if we cut this thing off early. That way, he can stay in the closet until he's ready, no harm done.

That part of me is quickly cut off by him leaning forward and pressing his mouth against mine. Like the first time, it feels like fire, and as his tongue enters my mouth, that fire turns into an inferno. Ravi's under my skin, and it's a feeling I never want to give up.

Screw it, I'm willing to fuck around with this soccer-playing hottie for a little more, even if I have to be in the closet with him.

We kiss and kiss, and my body is aching for him. I pull apart to catch my breath and hold his face with my hand. "I know what I wanna do for the rest of the night," he says, voice laced with lust.

I want to get fucked by him so bad, but I haven't prepped

my ass at all. On top of that, there's the other logistics of where we would go. My roommate is probably hanging out in our dorm right now. Should we fuck in my car?

As if to read my thoughts, he says, "My suitemates are all out at a bar, or home for the weekend. I was thinking we could go back to my room and I could... um..."

"Tell me what you want, Ravi," I reply, my voice husky with anticipation. *Please say what I'm hoping you're going to say.*

"I want to do what you did to me last time. I want to taste you, Steven."

Fucking jackpot.

19: Ravi

As I lead Steven up the stairs in the athletics dorm, I try to push down my nerves. I had just told him I wanted to taste him, that I wanted to return the sexual favor. While that was definitely still true, now I need to deliver, and the pressure is on.

"I like your suite," he says cheerfully as we walk into the common area. Our suite, like most in this building, has a large couch, one bathroom, and four single bedrooms, each with their own lock (thank God). "I expected it to be filled with like, smelly cleats and grass stains or something."

"Well we have a 24/7 robot housekeeper who gets the stains out," I joke. He giggles as I lean against my door.

"You said everyone's away?"

"Yup. They said they won't be back until 12." I check my phone, trying to hide the shakiness in my hands. "We have about 90 minutes or so to do... whatever..." I let my voice trail off as I turn to unlock my door and walk in.

I hear the click of my door closing as I put my jacket in the closet, still turned away. "Um, you can just have a seat anywhere and-" As I turn around, I'm cut off by the fact that Steven is right behind me, centimeters from my face.

I gasp and he smirks at me. His eyes are filled with mixture of longing and challenging lust as he looks down at my lips and back at my face. "Ravi," he growls at me.

"Steven."

"Did you mean what you said before? About how you wanted this night to end?"

"With you, I always mean what I say."

"Look," he says, his face softening. "You're new to all of this, I know that. We can take this as slow as you want." He says the words, but his eyes keep darting to my lips, betraying the meaning. It's written all over his face what he really wants. I'm nervous as hell, but I want to give it to him. I'm aware that I'm new to all this, but I want Steven to be my first everything.

"I know what I want Steven," I whisper, my breath touching his lips. "I want you, naked."

His eyes flare up and he smiles with delight. He steps back and I immediately start unbuttoning my shirt. When I get all the way down, I look up to see him shuck his off in a fast motion. My heart beats even faster and heat pools down into my crotch as I see him wearing the tight black tank top that I like.

"You okay?" He's smirking at me. He knows what he's doing to me, and I hope he never stops.

"Fan-fucking-tastic." I reach for his belt and yank him closer to me. I catch him with my lips and moan. While we kiss, his hands explore my back, and soon enough, they hungrily trail down to my ass. Even over my jeans, feeling him palm me is thrilling. Everything with Steven is like discovering the greatest wonders in life for the first time.

Our kisses start to get frantic, and my hands desperately start to undo his belt. I place kisses down his jaw and neck, then he moans. Just like last week, his skin tastes so good. I kiss his left shoulder and down his perfect arm for a bit. Finally, I pull his tank top up and off to reveal his cute little pecs and tight abs.

I've seen so many of my peers in peak athletic condition, most of them naked; not one of them was nearly as sexy to me as Steven. Not to sound redundant, but his body is a work of art.

Right now, it's more like a feast, and I'm a starving man.

Remembering his moves from last week, I lean in to catch his nipple with my mouth. He moans a higher pitch than I'm used to, and it has this primal effect on me. I switch to the other side and I hear him struggling in an effort not to howl. We'll see if I can get him screaming yet. I undo his pants then pull them down.

"Let me get on the bed," he whispers breathlessly. I nod and stand up. He pulls down the rest of his pants and his red boxer briefs along with the rest of his shoes and socks. I undo my own pants, as this is all getting way too hot.

Once I'm down to my own boxers, I turn around and am once again left stunned; Steven O'Rourke is lying on my bed, elbows propped up, and he's stroking his rock hard cock.

It's show time, now or never.

I lean close to him and kiss him, tongue meeting his. When I pull back, he looks at me, almost concerned. "We can do whatever you want, Ravi."

"Is it alright if I..." I reach his cock. I grasp it gently, and it pulses slightly in response. "Suck you off?"

His eyes roll back and his jaw goes slack. It would be adorably hilarious if I wasn't so horny as well. "Yes please," he pleads in a whimper.

I smile then move down to kiss his thighs, left then right. Then I lick at just the base near his balls while stroking him off slowly. This has the effect of him flopping back, hands on his face.

"Let me know how I'm doing okay?"

"Fuck...okay," he sighs. I love hearing him like that.

I lick a stripe all the way up to the tip. "Is this alright?"

"Yeah," he replies, barely in a whisper. His chin is tilted upward, and his breathing is rapid.

Finally, I take him in. He's not too big, so he fits in my mouth quite nicely. I'm trying to mind my teeth and use my tongue, hoping to give it to him good. I'm crazy self-conscious, but when he starts moaning and threading his hands through my hair, my insecurities go away.

The combination of tasting him, feeling him, and hearing him is turning me on like crazy. I use my left hand to palm my hardness through my boxers, all the while working him over with my mouth.

After what feels like both forever and not enough time, I hear him gasping, "Rav... I'm gonna... I'm gonna..."

"Give it to me," I think to myself. *"I want all of my firsts to be with you. I want you in my mouth, Steven O'Rourke."*

He moans one last time and then I'm overwhelmed with the taste of him. It's kind of salty, kind of weird, honestly, but hearing him moan gets me off. I swallow it down like a protein shake and slow down my sucking motions. Finally, I pull off and wipe my mouth.

I crawl into bed next to him. Seeing him strung out like this, breathing heavily and sweating- it makes it all worth it. All the awkwardness we went through, all the comfort zone shattering, all of it led me to this: having Steven in pure sexual bliss. It's almost as good as the orgasm he gave me the last time.

I pull off my boxers and begin to jerk myself off. I only go for a moment before Steven pushes my hand away and takes over, stroking me while grinning. After fifteen seconds, I thrust and grunt, ejaculating all over his side. My eyes flutter and I collapse, gasping. My bed's a mess and I don't even care. When I'm with Steven, so little concerns me.

He turns to me and kisses me. We lay there for some time, kissing and fading in-and-out of consciousness, bathing in the euphoria of post-orgasmic satisfaction.

"How was that?" I whisper.

"What was your word? Fan-fucking-tastic? Or was that three words?" We both giggle facing each other in my bed.

"I should get going," he finally says. "Your roommates will be back soon."

"Are you sure you don't want to stay? Maybe they won't notice." It's a lie, but I want to be with him so badly, I can't help it.

"Maybe. Maybe not." He gets up and starts to pick up his clothes. "But hey, let's call this incentive. If you come out to them, I can stay overnight all the time."

I sit up and smile. "You're saying you'd wanna do this again?"

"I'm saying I've had a good time these past two dates."

"And you wanna keep dating?" I'm beaming and my eagerness is showing, but I don't even care.

"If you're not sick of me yet." He's blushing as he puts on his clothes. I can tell all of this is making him almost as nervous as me.

I stand up and pull him into another kiss and a hug. The butterflies are still there, as always.

"I could never get enough of you."

I pull back to see a soft smile on his face, like he's thinking about a thousand things. He looks down, then looks back up. "Until next week then?"

"Next week then." I nod. I'll be counting the minutes.

20: Steven

"Next week" ends up being a lot more than that. Ravi forgot that he had an away game next Saturday and ends up getting back to campus really late that night. I guess it slipped his mind after he gave me the best blow job I've ever had (not that I have many men to compare him to). His first time going down on a guy went WAY better than my first time did, and I'm one-percent jealous, one-percent impressed, and 98-percent satisfied but hungry for more.

My desire to be with him intimately made the past week-and-a-half frustrating. We can't seem to find any more time to hook up. Between his practices, games, and classes, and with my roommate being around, we rarely get to physically see each other.

It's so, SO tempting to touch him in art class, but being discrete is important. Even if we were both out, class is not the time to be doing public displays of affection. Meanwhile, I still refuse to give Simone any details, a fact she is not happy about.

We text even more now, and I thought he'd be sick of my stupid memes and jokes, but he genuinely seems to enjoy communicating with me. We laugh together in-person and over the phone, and he brightens my day with *"good morning"* texts and *"goodnight"* messages as well. It's been so long since a guy has wanted this with me. I know he's closeted and I should be taking a step back, but between the hot sex and constant, genuine affection I've been getting, I feel myself falling for the co-captain of the soccer team, hard.

--

Today is Thursday, my slowest day, and my friends have been begging me to hang out. I feel obligated to go instead of sneaking around with Ravi, because, frankly, I haven't seen them in a while. Halloween is right around the corner, and I need to talk plans with them.

We agree to meet at the student union food court for dinner. As I walk toward the building, I get a text, and seeing it's from Ravi, I'm already smiling.

Ravi: *"Midterms are done. I need a friggin break."*
Me: *"Congrats! (smiley face)"*
Ravi: *"What are u up to?"*
Me: *"About to get dinner with some people. U?"*
Ravi: *"I'm starving. Could go for some food court Chinese."*
Me: *"That's actually where I am, lol."*
Ravi: *"Can I invite myself? (winking face)"*
Me: *"Well I'm gonna be with some friends."*
Ravi: *"The more the merrier."*
Me: *"Wut?"*

129

* * *

At this point, I'm texting while walking inside the food court. I keep spamming Ravi's phone, trying to find out if he's serious, but to no response. Our chatting in art class is one thing, but him being with my friends is new territory. How should I introduce him? We're not boyfriends yet, right? Can I put my arm around him? What do I do?

"Hey man." I look up and see Simone walking up to me holding a tray. "Jenny and the others are waiting for us, they nabbed a table."

"Uh, cool."

"You look stressed."

"I'm just uh…" I look down at my phone. No response. "Trying to decide what kind of food I wanna get."

Simone looks at me like she doesn't believe me. "Well, we'll be waiting for you out there." She proceeds to pick up a sandwich and pay.

I decide to get on the line to get some Chinese food. After the server gives me a tray of fried rice, out of the corner of my eye, I see a familiar figure wearing our school's official track suit for athletes. Ravi jogs up to me, barely stopping to get a tray, and he's huffing, like he just finished sprinting.

"Hey you," he smiles at me. Damn he looks good.

"Hey." I'm still in shock so I whisper, "What are you doing here?"

"Just getting some general tso's chicken." He grins at me and puts his tray on the glass for the server to place his food on.

"I'm meeting with my friends."

"So? I was hungry." He continues to smirk at me. "Do you not want me to sit near you?"

"It's not that."

"Do you not want them to meet me?" He's starting to sound genuinely offended.

"No I do!" I reply quickly.

"Well good then. Come on. You can say that I bumped into you while getting food." He smirks again and walks away to go pay.

Ravi hasn't told me he wants to be seen in public dating a guy. I don't want to accidentally out him, even though my friends are all pretty gay on some level. I promised to respect him being in the closet, but this is a big deal. I can barely handle being in art class without groping him, so how am I going to get through dinner with my friends without giving us away?

--

I walk up to the table where my friends are seated. It's in a corner, and thankfully, no other tables are around to eavesdrop. They're deep in mealtime conversation when I walk up, and Simone looks up at me. When she looks behind me to see Ravi, her eyes light up.

"Oh HEY Ravi!" Her tone is laced with insinuation, so I glare at her.

"Hey!" He nods at her.

"I bumped into him on line to get food!" I blurt, defensively.

"Oh yeah definitely," nods Simone, not buying it. She quickly gets up and grabs a free chair and adds it to the end of the table, and opens it motioning for Ravi to come sit. Now I'm sitting across from her, and Ravi is between us, looking at my four friends at the table. Absolutely perfect.

"Oh uh, guys, this is Ravi. Ravi, this is Dominic, Val, and Jenny. And of course, Simone."

"He's in our art class," Simone beams at the others. Jenny

gives a knowing nod while Val and Dominic simply wave.

"We were just prepping for our Halloween party this weekend," says Jenny. "I'm going as the Evil Queen, and Val's going as the Queen of Hearts."

"Yes, but can we talk logistics?" interjects Val. "I'm doing a liquor store run tomorrow. Beer, vodka, rum, or tequila?"

"Let's do it all," replies Dominic. "I'll chip in." His voice is deep compared to the girls, but he acts like a big old teddy bear.

"Me too, of course," I reply. I turn to Ravi and say, "They all live together in a house."

"And everyone in the house is gay or lesbian!" points out Simone. I send her another death glare.

"I prefer the terms ace or demi," says Jenny.

"Oh right, sorry." Simone turns to Ravi. "Like I said, I run with mostly queer people, so this house party is going to fabulous. So gay. Almost too gay!" She laughs and, to my relief, Ravi laughs with her, all while eating. He seems actually at ease.

"No such thing," retorts Dominic. "Though we will definitely be making fruity cocktails."

"That sounds amazing," replies Ravi. "Fruit-flavored drinks are the shit, people sleep on them."

"You get it!" laughs Dominic. "But of course, we're also doing jello shots."

"Speaking of shots, did you buy the mixers and the gelatin mix?" asks Val.

"Relax, hot stuff, I bought it last weekend," shrugs Dominic.

"Sounds like you're putting in a lot of work," Ravi comments. "I'm sure it's gonna be a party for the ages."

I look at Simone and I know she can read my mind, but she

replies anyway. "You should come! Steven is definitely coming, so you'll be among friends." It feels like every word she says is laced with implication, and my face is getting redder.

"He can't! Soccer and all that," I explain quickly.

"Actually I'm free next weekend. We won our last two games, so we actually have the weekend off. It's my last Saturday free for a while." His eyes dart to me for a moment. It's like he's asking me something, but I'm not sure what.

"Then we'll see you there!" Simone is way too cheerful at this.

"He still has to think about it." I raise my eyebrows at Simone and hope my tone conveys how much I want her to back off.

"I'm in!" Ravi grins. "I'll even chip in for drinks," he adds, pointing at Val.

"Oh thank you," replies Val, visibly relieved.

"Do you know what you're going as?" Jenny asks.

"I don't know." His voice trails off and his eyes dart to me again. I can tell he needs my help to decide.

"I can help you with a costume," volunteers Dominic. Hell no.

"No I got this, thank you!" I say quickly, turning to my right. Dominic is no flirt, but I'm cutting this off before it starts. I turn back to my left. "I'll find you something."

"What a great friend you are, Steven," Simone remarks, grinning like a maniac. "Hey, Ravi, maybe you can go as, like, a jungle boy- just a loincloth, no shirt, REAL authentic."

Ravi giggles at this and I continue my series of death stares at Simone. "I think we can do better than that," I mutter, gritting my teeth.

"I disagree," chuckles Dominic.

I turn to glare at him too when I hear Ravi push his chair out. "Well I'll see what we can come up with. It was nice meeting you all." Apparently he's done eating, so he gets up to put his tray on a nearby trash can. "Hey Steven, text me the address for Halloween?"

"Uh sure!"

"Steven, why don't you just carpool?" asks Simone.

"Oh that'd be great, that way I don't have to take the bus!" replies Ravi before I can respond.

"And since you're probably gonna be too drunk to drive home, just stay the night, both of you! We have a spare mattress and plenty of room!" The look I throw at Simone is borderline murderous.

"Can't wait!" Ravi replies, smiling. He waves and walks away quickly.

I look down at my tray of rice and start pushing some grains around with my fork. A part of me softens at the idea of him being friendly with my group. Deep down, I'm looking forward to partying with him, even if we don't get to spend the night having sex or anything like that. It's just nice to know that he can mingle with the people I hang out with and we won't have to hide our feelings for each other. Though we are going to be on a spare mattress together, alone. Maybe sex is ALSO a possibility?

I guess I'm looking down for too long, because I hear Jenny clear her throat and I look up. The others are all grinning at me now in silence.

"What?" I say, blushing I'm sure.

"Dude, you've got it bad," Dominic says.

They all burst out laughing. "Did you see his face just now?" screeches Simone. "All dreamy and everything!"

I hate my friends sometimes, but I legitimately can't wait for Saturday.

21: Ravi

I hear two rings over the phone and a voice answers. "Hello?"

"Hi Mom," I reply. It's Saturday afternoon, Halloween, and I'm right outside my dorm, talking on my cell.

"Ravi, honey." Her voice is warm with pleasant surprise. "To what do I owe this call?"

"We haven't spoken in two weeks."

"Yes, well you've been busy with soccer."

"And you've been busy with work trips," I counter.

"Yes, that's true. It seems like I'm on the road six days a week." My mom is in pharmaceutical sales. She's bright and good at talking people up. I just sometimes wish she knew how to turn off that charming, false tone when she talked to me. Our apartment is so far from school that she rarely gets to see me in person 10 months out of the year. "How are things?"

"Things are..." I pause for a moment. "Things are actually really great." For once it's true.

"You sound a little tired honey, I don't want you to lie to me. I may not be around but you can be honest."

"I am."

"Are you in trouble? Do you need money?"

"No." I roll my eyes. That's been her go-to method of mothering since I was a junior in high school.

"I can hear you rolling your eyes at me."

"Ha ha, well I'm not."

"Well then what's this call about?"

"I wanted to check in. You're still coming next weekend?"

"Yes, actually, there are some clients not too far from your university, so I'm driving down and everything. Are you still on to have a game?"

"So far so good. The season has been going pretty well." We continue to catch up for a bit before I bid my goodbye. I want to tell her I'm gay SO badly, but coming out over the phone doesn't feel right. It will have to be next week. I just hope I have the courage to face her when the time comes.

I walk back up to my suite and open the door to hear Landon.

"Which is why The Mousetrap is gonna be lit: with all the chicks in costumes, it's the place to be!" I walk in to see him standing up, gesturing wildly to Omar who's sitting on the couch, eating a bowl of cereal.

"You just want me to wingman you," he replies, mouth full of food. "Help you get some."

"Like I need help." Landon laughs nervously, but I know that's exactly what he wants. "Ravi, you're coming right?"

"Uh, can't," I say, scratching my head. "I have other plans."

"Ugh!" Landon scoffs in disgust. "Don't tell me you're still bailing on us for your mystery chick."

I look down so as to not make eye contact with either of them. I'm saved by Kareem who walks in and says, "Speaking of, here you go." He hands me a white button-down shirt on a hanger. "Wash it before you return it."

"No doubt, thanks bro."

"White-collar shirts?" Landon asks. He takes out his fingers and begins counting. "You never come out with us, you're always leaving in a hurry, you're going on mystery dates every Saturday. What happened to you man? What's so great about this girl?"

I try to muster up the courage to defend myself with some lie, but I'm interrupted by Omar, standing up. "Give it a rest, Sherlock. Ravi doesn't need to explain his personal life to you."

"Word, just drop it," chimes in Kareem, putting on his coat. "Now are we going to get pre-game supplies or what?"

Landon eyes me warily, before turning his attention to Kareem and following him out the door. As they walk out into the hall, I hear him asking, "Okay, so which of those cheerleaders did you invite?"

When I enter my room, I'm stopped from closing the door by Omar. I look at him and he's grinning.

"So, things must be going well with this mystery... person."

My face burns as I say, "Life is good. Nothing else to confirm or deny." At this point I'm rearranging things on my desk that don't need to be touched.

"Look, I can't cover for you forever, and you should take your time... but..." he trails off. I look up and see he's actually a bit nervous.

"What?"

"Are you... are- are you like..." he's stuttering. "Do you know what you're doing? With um... with like..."

What's he getting at?

His face turns red and he says, "Just make sure you do your research when it comes to, like, sex stuff. It's more than just use condoms. And lube. So, so much lube."

My eyes are blown wide. "Mhmm," is all I manage to mutter.

"Okay!" Omar nods, while looking up. "Good talk."

"Yup!" I squeak.

As he turns to leave, his words mill around in my mind. Steven is picking me up in four hours. I guess I should fire up the internet and do some research.

--

Hours later, I'm walking down to meet Steven at his car. I'm wearing a jacket, black jeans and the white button-down Kareem let me borrow. Steven told me he to wear a shirt like this and that he'd take care of the rest of the costume. Surprises typically gave me anxiety, but with him, I've learned to just go with it; all my fears subside when Steven's around, and he hasn't steered me wrong yet.

I meet him near the campus parking lot, we nod and exchange greetings, then walk down. He's wearing a black hoodie, but otherwise I can't tell anything about his supposed costume. It must be in the big black duffel he's got slung over his shoulder.

"What's in the bag?" I ask.

"Oh just some supplies. Val asked me to bring something edible for twelve people that's not dripping in alcohol, so I bought some apple cider doughnuts earlier."

139

"That can't be everything in there."

"There are …other things." He smirks at me.

"Oh? What kind of things?"

"Some spare toothbrushes in case we stay over." He pauses to look at me while we walk. "And condoms and stuff." He winks and my eyes are blown wide.

We get to the car and I'm trying not to freak out visibly. He starts the engine and turns to me, grinning.

"I was just kidding about the condoms. There are like 20 doughnuts in here."

I nod and lean over, my breath on his face. I kiss him, tenderly, just a teasing taste of what I really want. "I hope you're not kidding," I growl. Steven makes me so horny without even trying, I want him to know that I'm game.

There's a sparkle in his eyes and he reaches back to rummage through his back seat. Is he whipping out sex stuff right now?

Instead, he undoes his sweater to reveal a tight red sleeveless shirt. He's managed to grab a plastic headband with red devil horns and white one with a sparkly pipe-cleaner in a round shape, and my face immediately falls. "Oh no," I groan.

"Oh yes." He puts the white headband on me. "You're my angel tonight." He puts the red devil horns on himself.

"I can't believe you," I laugh. I'm trying to pout but it's not working, this whole situation is too cute.

"I told you I'd get you a costume."

"You're a menace to society." I chuckle at him, still trying to frown.

"A demon more like it." He winks and flicks his red plastic horns. We both giggle while he pulls out of the parking spot.

--

140

15 minutes later, we arrive at a residential street. I see a lot of people walking toward what I presume to be Simone's house. It's a large two-story fixture with a private lawn, almost like a cleaned-up haunted house (how appropriate).

I turn to my left and see Steven looking at his steering wheel, thrumming with nerves.

"What's up?"

"Um, so like… There's gonna be a lot of gay guys at this party."

"Oh. I figured. I don't care what they think about me. They can start rumors, I don't give a shit."

"Yeah, but, like…" Steven shrugs, biting his lip. "They're probably gonna, you know… hit on you. 'Cause you're hot, and you totally can hook up with whomever you want. We never said we were exclusive, and- and- and," he stammers.

Oh. Oh this is what he's concerned about? I put my hand on his then place it on his thigh.

"Steven, I'm not flirting with anyone else," I smile. He finally looks up at me, still concerned. He's so cute. "The only one I want to hook up with is you."

"Really?"

"I'm dating you. I only want to date you."

He beams at me, and I know I responded the right way. He pauses for a moment then looks down. "You know what else I really want?" he asks.

I look at him puzzled, then he kisses me hard. His tongue sweeps mine and his lips are just as addictive as ever. He kisses down my jaw then whispers into my ear, "I want you to fuck me. Tonight." He gives my ear a quick nibble and goosebumps shiver down my spine while my eyes close.

After he pulls away, I stare at him. When I don't reply, his grins slowly fades. "But only if you're ready."

I smile back. "We've got a party to get to!" I get out of the car so fast I'm shaking.

22: Steven

The Halloween party is amazing. Val's planning ability is really shining, and with all the decorations the rest of us put into it, plus the drinks Dominic is concocting, I can feel everyone really enjoying themselves. We're all decked out in amazing and colorful costumes. There's a sea of ballgowns, superhero suits, and wigs of pink, green, and blue. The living room area has the bass booming as someone has hooked up mini-speakers to their streaming device. The table has been cleared to make way for water pong, where, if you fail, you take a sip of whatever drink tickles your fancy. All the guests are raving about Dominic's specialty punch, which, frankly, is a little too strong for me, but it seems to relax Ravi.

Speaking of, I see him in the front area playing a card game with a drink in hand. He's sitting next to Simone, Jenny, and some guy in an elaborate pirate costume. They're all drinking and laughing; it warms my heart to see him so comfortable with my friends.

"Your heart-eyes are showing," sings Dominic, who's mixing a fresh batch of punch. I'm standing in the sequestered kitchen area with him.

"What?"

"Your couples costume is cute, too." He proceeds to put (literally) an entire bottle of vodka into the bowl.

"I think I'm going to make things 'boyfriend' official soon."

"What a surprise," he deadpans.

"Really?"

"No!" Dominic laughs. "You see the way that Greek god looks at you?"

"He is really hot." I giggle as I look over to him. He's swapping cards with Simone and smiling.

I take another sip of my punch and grimace. "Bro, these are so strong!" I laugh. "I need to stop, I don't wanna get smashed."

"Why not?"

"Well..." I look around to make sure no one's watching. Recognizing this as the universal sign of impending gossip, Dominic leans in. "I haven't eaten all day if you catch my drift."

"What? Why not?"

I glare at him. "You know exactly why not. You've bottomed before, haven't you?"

"Oh!" He nods. "Well lucky you."

"Not lucky yet," I murmur into my cup. I take a sip and see Ravi in the distance. He's smiling, and he looks at me and nods.

"Just please clean up. I don't want like, semen stains in our attic."

"Dude, gross!" I laugh.

"Hey, you're the one hooking up in OUR house." He picks up a cup of water. "Now switch to water and go eat some carbs, please."

I giggle and put down my punch, walking away with the new cup. I pick up a doughnut and proceed to mingle. Halloween is the best night of the year.

--

It's about 2 o'clock when mostly everyone leaves and the party starts to die down. Ravi and I slip away while I mention to Simone that we're going to sleep on the spare mattress in the attic. I've slept over before, so I know how to get up there and access the bedding. The attic area is surprisingly comfortable (and totally private). I take my time, allowing Ravi to brush his teeth first so I can move some stuff around. Now the mattress has some bedsheets and even a spare comforter- not bad for drunk undergrads.

After Ravi returns, I go downstairs to brush up as well. I even use a few wipes to make myself extra clean all over. No pressure, but I need Ravi's first time to be fucking phenomenal. After giving myself a small pep talk in the mirror, I climb back up the stairs to the attic.

Walking up there, I stop dead in my tracks at the sight: Ravi is sprawled out on the mattress, naked and hard. He's stroking himself slowly while looking directly at me.

"You coming?" His voice is growly and commanding.

"Make me," I reply, threateningly, while I rip my shirt off. He giggles and gets up to kiss me while holding my hips.

He pulls me down into the mattress and I giggle onto his mouth while fumbling to take my own pants off. I pull apart for a moment to step out of my pants and reach down to pull out two packets of lube and a chain of condoms.

Ravi smiles and leans to kiss my neck. "I actually brought condoms too, just in case," he murmurs into my skin. This has the effect of making me shiver and getting me hard.

"Well aren't we both prepared," I hiss, eyes closed, as he kisses down to my chest. "Good to know you- ah, ah… you had the same ideas as me… FUCK!" How can I talk with this stud trailing kisses on every part of my body?

"I have plenty of ideas." He flicks my nipples (right, then left) with his tongue and I cry out. "But I'll need to use the condom to do it."

I nod and hand one to him. He gets up and strokes his large dick. I lay back, naked, and open up a packet of lube.

"I'm so glad we're doing this," he moans, while rolling the condom on.

"I'm the luckiest guy in the world right now, 'cause I have you, and you're hot as hell," I moan while I start to finger myself with the lube.

"No, I'm pretty sure I'm the lucky one." He strokes himself and leans forward over me.

"We can either argue about this forever, or you can get inside me." He giggles and catches my lips.

"The second one."

"Agreed," I murmur back into his lips. I use three fingers to open myself up now. "I'm ready."

He smiles and leans back, lining himself up with my hole. My legs are spread wide and I take his dick and guide it a bit with my hands.

As he pushes inside me, his face contorts into visions of shock and pleasure. There's that familiar discomfort, but seeing his face thrills me. "Keep going, please," I beg.

That's all it takes. Ravi proceeds to enter me further, and pull out, moaning each time. I'm well lubed, so it's a pretty easy ride. As he thrusts, I match him with my sounds of pleasure, and groaning "Fuck yeah."

It feels so good to have him inside me that any discomfort subsides pretty quickly. Eventually his speed ramps up. He's strong (REALLY strong) and his muscles tense in such a sexy way, I can't help but stare at him. He's working up a sweat and his eyes are closed as he hold my legs up and drills me into the mattress. I'm loving every moment of it.

After five more minutes, I stroke my hardness between us. Upon seeing this, Ravi goes animalistic. "Fuck yeah, you like this?" he growls.

"Yes. Don't stop."

"I won't," he grunts, panting.

"Keep going."

"I'm gonna…" His voice is a desperate plea now, teetering on the edge of collapse.

"Yes! Fuck me!"

"Fuuuck," he growls.

With one last thrust, I feel him pulse inside me. He's moaning and shivering for thirty seconds. I know it's his first time but DAMN he did it so well, it felt like my first time too.

After he pulls out and collapses next to me, it takes me all of five strokes before I'm moaning as well, coming all over myself. After a moment of seeing stars, I look over and see an expression of satisfaction on Ravi's face, inches away from mine.

I bask in the perfection of this moment in time and space: this attic, this mattress, this man next to me- all of it. Anal sex was only okay in the past, but THIS? This is sex with Ravi, sex with someone I'm really starting to fall for. This is

147

paradise.

23: Ravi

I wake up early, uncomfortable in a room that's not my own. I look down and see Steven's body draped over mine.

As memories of last night start to return, my thoughts begin to chant, *"I'm not a virgin, I'm not a VIRGIN, WOOHOO I'M NOT A VIRGIN ANYMORE!"*

After the initial cheering and congratulating myself on (FINALLY) getting laid in my head, I smile at seeing Steven peacefully sleeping. Last night was perfect, and if Steven's reactions were any indication, I'd say I performed pretty well. Most importantly, it was with someone I really cared about, and I know the other guys can't say that about their first times.

I feel Steven stir, and he finally lifts his head up and yawns. "Morning, you," he mutters. Even with bed head and five hours of sleep, he's still the most handsome man I've ever seen.

I don't want to say any of that, so instead I reply, "Morning gorgeous."

He smiles and blushes. "You this sweet to all the girls the morning after they have sex with you?"

"No girls. Or guys. Virgin remember?"

"Are you sure?" He grins and crawls up next to me, so we're eye level. "You did really well, it feels like you're a practiced professional."

"Practiced soccer player, yes. Sex person, no." I cringe inwardly at my lame-ass jokes. "It was my first time."

"Well you did great." He flops back down and stares at the ceiling. Light is streaming through a nearby window and there's a peaceful silence. It's not too shabby in this attic- I wonder if they'll let us stay here in this bubble forever. "I knew you were a virgin, and that was kind of a lot of pressure on me."

"Are you serious? The pressure was on me! You could've said and done nothing and I still would've enjoyed it."

"Comatose was an option? Dammit!" I shove him slightly and we both giggle.

"Ass."

"My ass is yours now," he replies. Our laughter dies down and he looks at me with a serious expression.

"What is it?"

"This is so stupid, but..." He wipes his face. "I still have this fear that now you're not going to want anything to do with me."

"What?" I'm in shock. What the hell is he talking about?

"Well the first guy I ever kissed wanted to hide everything about us. Sean, while it took a while, he got bored of me."

"You still think I'm gonna get bored of you? Or change my mind or whatever?"

Steven closes his eyes. "I know, it's stupid. I'm in my head with my dumb insecurities."

"Steven, I already told you: I'm never going to get bored of you."

"You're not just going to stop dating me now that I've put out?" He's looking me in my eyes and I see legitimate fear.

"Why would I stop dating you?"

"Well you're not out to most of your friends and teammates. Now would be a convenient time to cut things off from me."

"Steven, listen to me." I take his hand and kiss it. He looks at me with those gorgeous eyes filled with concern. "I want to keep dating you. As long as you'll have me."

He smiles and kisses my hand too. "Done deal, soccer captain."

"I was actually thinking about coming out to my mom."

"Really?"

"Yeah, but I wanna do it in person. She's visiting next week for my game."

"Well that's a huge deal." Steven leans up on his elbows to take a good look at me. His look is a mixture of shock, admiration, and concern. "How do you think it's going to go?"

"I don't know. She's always talked about me having a wife and kids some day. I think she's really looking forward to me having the traditional family. Me being gay might really crush the dreams she has for me."

I pause, but Steven just looks at me. It's a comfortable quiet. I take a deep breath and continue.

"We don't see each other much now that I'm in college. My dad died when I was little, and since then she's been working nonstop, driving all over the country selling pharmaceuticals." The words pour out as Steven curls up onto my chest. "She's close to my aunt, her sister, and she spends most holidays with them. I go with her for Christmas but typically I spend my holidays on campus or hanging out with Omar or Kareem's family. She's my mom, but we don't have much in terms of a family unit."

"Family can mean a lot of things," replies Steven.

"Yeah, but she's the only one I've got. It might break her heart finding out I'll never have a wife."

"Do you want me to come? Give you emotional support as your... guy you're seeing?"

It warms me to know he wants to help. I also note his distinct lack of the word *'boyfriend'*. "Thank you, but no. I don't want her to think you *'turned me gay'* or whatever. This is me, this has been a long time coming."

Steven nods and looks at me in the eyes. I pull him closer and give him a nice long, tender kiss. "But thank you, it means a lot to me that you're willing to help."

"Of course." His eyes twinkle. "I'll support you. You have me now, Ravi."

"I know." I smile back.

--

A week later, we finish our home game, where my mom is in the stands. It feels great to see her clapping along, paying attention to us on the field; I barely see her look down at her phone to answer emails or anything.

All in all, it's not too exciting of a game, but we do win as Omar scores the one goal in the entire game. I'm proud to note that Paul made the assist, and Landon and Kareem give him major props in the locker room afterward. It's great to see him and the others starting to get along so well.

After the game, my mom insists on taking me, Kareem, and Landon (Omar said he was busy) to get burgers for dinner because she claims she wants to get to know the friends I've been spending my Thanksgivings and spring breaks with. Dinner is perfectly pleasant with lots of small talk about college and Landon attempting to regale my mom with stories about our games. Kareem is polite and asks my mom about her job as a traveling pharmaceutical rep. As we eat, I feel the anxiety coming along as I want to finally come out to her, but not in front of the guys.

After she drops us off, I tell them I need to have a moment to talk to my mom. I get into the passenger seat and she looks at me. "What's up, honey?"

My heart is beating out of my chest. I've never been this nervous in my life, but it's now or never.

"Mom. I've come to terms with some things while I've been at university."

"Okay," she says, her tone urging me to go on.

"I realize, now, that... my life..." Just spit it out. "I'm not like Kareem and his girlfriend. I don't want a girlfriend. I like I'm probably gay."

After the longest five seconds of my life, my mom finally says, "You're... 'probably'?"

"No." I look down and shake my head. "I'm definitely gay. The guys don't know. But it's... it's the truth."

"Um..." I look at her to gauge her face. It's dark, but her face seems neutral. "What made you realize this?"

"I've known since I was a teenager. It's just who I am I guess."

"But... um..." I stare at her. I just want this to be okay. I just want to be who I am, and my mom needs to know.

She finally continues, "It's getting late sweetie, and I bet you're tired from the game."

"Yeah I suppose." I see her staring at the steering wheel.

"I'll be sure to stop by so we can get brunch. Are doughnuts okay?"

"I guess?" I shrug.

"Perfect. I have to umm… hit the road after lunch, so I'll text you when I'm outside your dorm. Maybe around 10?"

"Okay."

"Go get some sleep, honey."

After I unbuckle my seatbelt, she awkwardly tries to reach over to hug me but is tugged by her own seatbelt. We both give the most forced chuckle I've ever heard as she pulls back to unbuckle. Then, she leans over and hugs me.

"Love you mom," I mutter.

"Love you too sweetie," she whispers back. There's that at least.

24: Steven

Things have been going well for Ravi and I, but we haven't gotten to hang out or hook up at all this week. Saturday night he was so busy with the game and his mom that I didn't want to disturb him, other than a few texts offering my support. It's Sunday evening when I finally hear from him again. He texted me earlier this afternoon stating he was hanging out with his mom before she left. That was five hours ago, so I can only hope he's okay. Coming out isn't easy and I hope he followed through with it.

I'm walking out of my dorm when I get a call from him, and my heart is relieved. "Hey you," I say with a smile when I answer the phone.

"Hey what's up?"

"Not much. About to go get dinner soon then maybe go do some more work in the fine arts building."

"Oh, that reminds me, I haven't eaten in like 7 hours."

"Babe, this sounds like a food emergency." I wince internally at calling him a pet name, but Ravi just makes me want to be all couple-y, I can't help it. "I'm afraid I'm going to have to remedy this."

I hear him chuckle over the phone. "I wanted to talk to you in person, so this is perfect."

My anxiety levels rise but I try to ignore it. "Well I'll be in the union food court soon."

"Perfect. See you then... babe." I blush as I hang up the phone- I've been doing that a lot lately.

--

I'm sitting at a table in the back eating my pizza when I finally lock eyes on him. He seems more anxious than usual, but his plate is piled high with Chinese food, so I'm sure he's going to sit with me for a while. I smile and greet him as he sits down.

"How's life?" I ask, trying to tamp down my curiosity. "How was your day?"

"Well," he says, stuffing his face, "It was... I'm sorry, I'm just really hungry."

"No go on," I chuckle.

"You must think I'm a total pig."

"This is what I'm going to have to put up with from now on? An athlete's metabolism?" I chuckle at him, and something sparkles in his eyes.

"As long as you'll keep me around," he smiles. He takes a sip of his water and looks at me. I feel his foot graze mine. I think it's his way of holding hands or showing affection but keeping it private. I'll take it.

"What did you wanna talk about?"

"Well, I kinda wanted to talk about what happened

today." He shovels more general tso's chicken into his mouth.

"Yeah, how did things go with your mom?"

He looks around for a moment. No one is even near us, and very few people are facing us. "I'd rather continue this conversation outside somewhere, if it's alright with you?"

"Of course."

"How was your day, babe?" He smirks.

"Ugh," I fake grimace. "Are we really doing pet names?"

"Hey you started it," he retorts with a mouthful or rice.

We both laugh. Even though he doesn't want the team to know he's dating me, chatting with him and catching up makes me feel warm inside.

We small talk for 10 more minutes before he finishes his food. Afterwards, we walk together to an area near his dorm. There are some benches and trees, but it's mostly secluded, almost no dorms are nearby. As the sun is setting over the November sky, there's a chill in the air. I watch the way the twilight covers his face; staring at Ravi's perfect features is never going to get old.

I wait for a minute in silence before he begins. "I told my mom I'm gay."

"That's awesome! Right?"

"Yeah well. I don't know." He's not even looking at me and I can feel an uneasiness radiating off of him.

"What'd she say?"

"Well last night when I told her, she kind of didn't respond. Then today, she took me to lunch then grocery shopping. I kept waiting for her to bring it up but she never did. It was so frustrating, I was just waiting for the ball to drop."

Ravi continues to talk staring out at nothing at all. I want to hold him but I don't know if that's crossing too many

157

boundaries.

"Then finally, as she was leaving, I asked her if there was anything else she needed to say to me, and she just looked at me and said nothing."

"Really?"

"Yeah. Then I said, '*Nothing about me being, you know, gay?*' And you wanna know her response?"

"What?"

"She said, '*You're too young. You don't know what you want yet. I'm sure eventually you'll settle down with a girl.*' "

"No fucking way."

"Yeah," he whispers. His eyes are starting to well up now, and it's taking all of my strength to not hug him.

"That's bullshit."

"I know. I told her this is who I am and she just kinda... looked at me... with a weird look of pity almost. Then she made up some excuse saying she had to leave for her job and told me of her plans to go on some cruise with my aunt for Thanksgiving. Then she peace'd out."

"No fucking way," I whisper. "Ravi I'm sorry."

"I can't fucking believe this!" he barks up at the sky, scaring away some nearby birds. He buries his eyes in his palms. "My own mom won't even believe me."

"Ravi, I-" I'm interrupted by him pushing his face into my chest. I hear some sobs and feel him shivering. After the initial surprise, I wrap my arms around him like I've been wanting to.

"I don't get it," I hear him cry, muffled into my chest. "This was supposed to be the most important moment of my life."

"And it was," I say, rubbing his back. "I'm so proud of you, babe."

We stay there for what feels like an eternity, but was

probably only fifteen minutes. I rub his back while the shivers subside.

Finally, he gets up and wipes away his tears. "Sorry about all this." His eyes are puffy and red, but I don't blame him. Today was a big deal, and holding in all this emotion couldn't have been easy.

"Don't be sorry. You deserve to be heard and understood." I pat his head gently, trying to calm him. I want to be his strength, for now and the foreseeable future. "Your mom will come around. And we're gonna get through this."

"Thanks." He looks down at my lips and back up at me. "You must think I'm a total punk-ass for crying over nothing."

"Hey it wasn't nothing- your mom didn't accept you. That's awful and no one deserves that. And look- you came out! That's a big deal! Fucking phenomenal!"

"I know." A small glimmer of a smile begins to reappear. "But thanks anyway." He leans in and hugs me properly on the bench. "I knew I could count on you. You always make me feel better, even when I feel like shit."

"Hey, what are boyfriends for?" As soon as the word slips out, I immediately regret it. Ravi pulls away almost comically fast. Oh boy, this is going to get awkward.

"Did you say 'boyfriends'?"

"Uh... no?" I shrug.

"Did I...did I pass all the tests?" he chuckles. "Do I finally get to call you my boyfriend?"

"What?" My jaw nearly drops. "Tests? Ravi, you passed all the tests, like, the day we met. I just wasn't sure if you wanted to stick around with me!" We're both giggling now.

"Glad to hear I passed." His eyes once again flicker to my lips, but this time he leans in quickly to kiss me. I'm still stunned when he says, "Come with me back to my dorm? We can have a little more privacy in my room."

"But what about your teammates? Won't they suspect something?"

He stands up and offers a hand to pull me up. "They can talk all they like. Tonight I need to hold you. You're my boyfriend after all, Steven."

"Playing that card already, are we Mr. Metta?" I'm smirking at him as I stand up.

"Hey, I earned it, I might as well use it, Mr. O'Rourke."

--

We walk up the pathway to his dorm. Fortunately for us, none of his suitemates are around when we walk in. We spend the next several hours holed up in his room with the door locked. We're mostly cuddling in the bed, watching old shows on his laptop, chatting and giggling. In our various states of undress, our hands find each other, leading to the occasional swapped blowjob session. The only time we put on clothes is to take breaks to use the bathroom, and I'm grateful that his roommates don't catch me the entire time.

We sleep curled up in each other's arms, whispering words of gratitude and sharing how amazing the other person is. If sex with Ravi was fantastic, sleeping with him, sharing a bed with him, and spending the night- it's beyond words. It's the best I've ever felt.

25: Ravi

The next three weeks before Thanksgiving fly by, and yet take forever. Everyone on campus is bogged down with exams and projects, and my friends and I are no exception. Steven is busy preparing for his semester show; he's spending a lot of time surveying the off-campus studio that he was assigned, because apparently he's sharing the show and the space with three other artists.

We try to hang out as much as we can, but as usual, it's been difficult. Sometimes we get to have lunch with Simone and Jenny, and it's nice to share some public displays of affection in front of them. For those short meals, Steven and I can act like a real couple. Our flirty jokes via text never stop. Still, between practices and classes, we've only gotten to sleep together once in those weeks. That is not to say that we don't fool around- isn't that what his car is for? I swear, just getting into his back seat makes me horny these days.

Speaking of being busy, things are looking up for the team. We lost only one game, but since then we've been ramping up, winning each other one. The team morale is pretty high, and coach is proud that we're gelling so well. I may be sneaking around with a guy, but on the field I still command respect as co-captain.

--

The team is doing a calisthenics day one afternoon in the athletics center gym, about a week before Thanksgiving. Everyone is on a different machine, and I'm on a bench doing some bicep curls with a dumbbell when my phone vibrates. I already smile as I literally drop my weight and grab my phone, knowing it's a text from Steven.

Steven: *"This art history lecture is so boring, I've fallen into an eternal slumber, like sleeping beauty."*

Me: *"You want me to be the prince and kiss u to save u?"*

Steven: *"Anything to get a little affection. I haven't seen you in ages!"*

Me: *"Last night was ages huh? (winking face emoji)"*

Steven: *"Without you? Might as well be a DECADE."*

I'm smiling, about to reply, when I hear a familiar voice clear his throat behind me.

"Coach will have your ass if he catches you texting during practice." I turn to see Logan smirking at me. He's always around during our practices, cleaning up or taking inventory.

"Uh, sorry Logan." I scramble to put my phone away.

"No worries," he laughs. "I'm not your coach, even though I watch all your games. You did awesome on Tuesday, by the way, nice assists."

"Thanks."

162

"Today, though you seem distracted. You shouldn't be letting your guard down during these practices. The season isn't over."

"Uh, yeah."

"Look, when I was your age, I used to text and smile and blush- I know THAT kind of distraction."

"They had texting back in the 1950's?" shouts Landon, garnering laughs from most of the guys who are now listening to our conversation.

"It was the early 2000's, LANDFF, I ain't no old-timer!" he retorts, feigning offense. Everyone loves Logan, he really was just one of the guys.

"He's probably just texting his mystery girl," remarks Landon.

My eyes blow wide open. I look left and right, then chuckle nervously.

"Really?" asks Logan.

"Yeah. He won't introduce her to us, but he probably met her in the art class he has to take."

"Leave him alone, Landon," Omar chastises, getting up. "You're just pissed 'cause you have to take an arto class next semester."

A few guys laugh and Landon really starts to get mad. "My advisor is an idiot! And now who knows what class I'll be stuck in?"

"Now, now Landon," Logan starts, putting an arm around his shoulder and leading him back to the bench he was working out on. "It won't be so bad. Hell, maybe I'll join you. I get one free class a semester. I've always wanted to take up an instrument."

The two of them get in an argument about why Landon should never be allowed near music, while I breathe a sigh of relief. I look up to see Omar give me a knowing *"you owe me one"* look, and we all get back to our personal workouts.

--

Later that night I get a text from Steven that has me worried. He asks me if we could chat, and I try not to panic. I lie on my bed in just my boxers and dial him up.

"Hey," I hear him say over the phone.

"What's up?"

"Um, okay." He sounds nervous as he begins. "So I uh, wanted to ask you something."

"Okay." Just get on with it please!

"I heard you don't have any plans for Thanksgiving and that you were staying on campus. Thanksgiving with my family is always lame and stressful, but I was thinking..."

He's drawing out the question but I already want to say yes.

"Do you wanna like, maybe, come home with me for Thanksgiving break?"

"Yes!" I say immediately, smiling.

"No pressure if you can't or don't want to, or think it's too soon."

"You told me they know you're gay."

"I've been out since I was a preteen," he laughs.

"Right." I chuckle. "Do they know about us?"

"Uhh... I MAY have mentioned it to my mom. And she MAY be demanding I bring you around so she can meet you."

"Oh." The nerves are back again. This is a big deal.

"No pressure though! You can totally say no!"

"No, no, I mean... yes. I want to go."

"Really?"

"Yeah, absolutely." I'm trying to come off casual, but this

is a big deal. I know it's a lot of pressure but I want to be a part of Steven's life, not just at school but at home too. He has a big family and they're big supporters of his. "Beats staying on campus."

"I'll take that as a *'Yes, it is my duty as your boyfriend with the gorgeous smile to accompany you home and save you from annoying cousins.'* "

"You think I have a gorgeous smile?" I smirk.

"Alright Mr. *'Fishing-for-compliments'*, I gotta go." I hear him giggle as I laugh, telling him goodnight.

--

The day before Thanksgiving, we take the four-hour drive down to his childhood home. It's the longest car ride we've ever been in together, and it's pretty relaxing just listening to music and casually chatting, getting the scoop on all the family I'm going to meet. I don't have much in terms of extended family, so this is going to be quite an experience.

As the sun sets, we pull up into a suburban street and park near a large house. Now my nerves are really starting to get to me. It's actually happening. I'm meeting a boyfriend's parents. They know I'm gay and I'm sleeping with their son. Holy shit.

You'd think someone who's played with over a thousand people in the stands watching me, cheering my name (or booing me during away games) would be used to the pressure, but this is another level entirely.

"Hey," Steven says from the driver's seat, pulling me back down to Earth. I turn to my left to look at him. He puts his hand on my thigh. "You okay?"

"Yeah. Yeah. Yeah," I stutter, staring at the house again, trying to relax. "Totally. Yeah."

165

"Look, Ravi, I'm here for you. You're my boyfriend." I turn back to look at him. His eyes are warm and kind, and his tone is soothing. I'm immediately reminded that Steven has the power to calm me down. "And my family is going to love you, I promise."

"What if they don't?" I ask, concern etched on my face.

"Then I'll beat 'em up." He smiles and leans in to kiss me on the cheek. I giggle as he opens his door. "Come on, dinner's almost ready."

--

As we walk in with our bags, I'm met with the sounds of a busy kitchen, the delicious scent of celery, carrots, and baked meat, and the noises of kids' cartoons down the hall. Steven had prepped me for such, but it's still jarring. When I went home it was nearly always silent, even if my mom was there
.

"Hey mom," announces Steven, as he puts his bags down and rounds into the kitchen. I follow closely and see an older woman by the stove as she turns around to greet Steven. She's slender, with gray-and-brown hair, and the same kind eyes as the boy of my dreams. She looks over at me and I try to give my least nervous smile.

"And hello! You must be Ravi!"

"Yeah, um, uh hi," I stutter while she wraps her arms around me. Hugging is something that also almost never happens in the Metta household. "Nice to meet you Mrs. O'Rourke."

She steps back and gives me an appraising look up and down. "Wow I see you brought home a real athlete, son."

"Mom," whines Steven, his face turning a shade darker.

"I'm just glad you boys made it home safely." She turns

and looks to me. "You know he barely calls me anymore. I think something ELSE has been taking up all his time." She gives me a knowing look and I almost chuckle.

"OKAY! Um, we're gonna unpack our bags. Where are the twins?" asks Steven, desperately trying to get us out of there.

"Your brother is with them in the living room. Dinner will be ready in a few minutes. Hope you like chicken!"

"Yes ma'am," I reply, as Steven walks through the kitchen area to the living room.

As I follow him, I hear the sounds of cartoons before I see the kids. Two adorable red-haired girls are sitting down with dolls in their lap watching an animated program about a princess and a talking snowman. There are toys littered everywhere and one soft lamp illuminates the room.

On a nearby couch sits presumably Steven's brother, reading a book.

"Hey. Twin duty?" whispers Steven, so as to not interrupt the girls' movie.

"Yup. Getting some reading done," replies his brother not even looking up.

"What reading? It's the day before Thanksgiving."

"Trigonometry 1 never takes a day off, brother," he deadpans. He finally looks up and his eyebrows jump for a minute when he spots me. "Oh."

"Hey," I greet him.

"This is Ravi," adds Steven. "Ravi, my brother Sly."

"Nice to meet you," I shake his hand. If he had told me they were identical twins, I'd believe it. Where Steven is dangling hair and an eyebrow piercing, Sly is slicked-back hair and glasses. His demeanor is different but their faces are so alike-that's genetics for you.

"Likewise."

"Trigonometry is no joke, I get why you're studying," I remark.

"You're taking it?"

"Freshman year I did. It involved a lot of reading on team busses to games."

"Oh!" He turns to Steven between us. "So you really did manage to bring home a soccer player?"

"Why do people keep saying that?" he asks, indignantly. Sly and I both giggle at his expense.

After a few more minutes, we hear Steven's mom holler that dinner is ready. I watch as Sly and Steven (both the same height) each escort one of the twins to the dining area. As I make my way to my designated seat, I pray inside that this weekend continues to go as smoothly as it has been. Just maybe, in the long run, I'll get to be part of this family for real.

26: Steven

That first dinner goes really well, all things considered. The twins are on their best behavior, and Ravi seems really comfortable the whole time. When my dad and Shannon arrive a little bit later, we continue to have dinner with them after they shower and join us. Sly immediately rushes off back to twin duty while the rest of my family gently asks Ravi several probing (but not too pressing) questions. At one point I turn to look at him and give him a silent *"you okay?"* look with my eyes and he seems really comfortable.

Later that night, in my childhood bedroom (the one I share with my little brother), we unpack our bags. I notice the sleeping bag and several pillows my mom had set up for Ravi. It was a valid gesture considering we don't have a guest bedroom, and Sly and I both have twin beds.

Once we're done changing into our pajamas, I find it telling that Sly is nowhere to be found. Ravi and I are talking, sitting

169

down in his little make-shift floor-bed, when Sly walks in the room. He pointedly doesn't look at us, scurrying to grab a few things from his side of the room, including a pillow.

"Hey, you going to bed soon?" I ask, from the floor.

"Um yeah," he replies, still not looking at us. It's not like we're naked or anything, so I'm wondering why he's acting like this. "I have um, a lot of studying to do, so I might just pass out on the basement couch, no big deal." He dashes away before I can argue.

After a moment, Ravi and I giggle at his blatant lie. We shut the lights off a few minutes later. We lay there in silence basking in the glow of the moonlight. When it's clear that Sly's not coming back, I manage to convince Ravi to curl up next to me in my tiny twin.

"Are you sure?" asks Ravi, spooning against me. "It's not exactly comfortable."

"I don't care." My voice is muffled against the wall. "I want you wrapped around me as much as possible. My brother's clearly not coming back tonight."

"I feel bad. Like we 'sexiled' him."

"We are SO not having sex tonight," I giggle.

"Shh." His laughter vibrates against my back. "Your parents might hear."

"Might hear us NOT having sex?"

"I'm trying to be a good little boyfriend and impress your parents," he whispers.

Hearing this warms my heart. "I think you already have. Now be a good boyfriend and help me sleep."

"How so?"

"Just hold me. I sleep better with you cuddled up near me."

"Me too," he yawns. With that, slumber overtakes me, and being cramped in my old twin bed has never felt so good.

--

There's not too much to do Thanksgiving morning. My parents insist I take Ravi out so they can prepare our family's holiday lunch. Shannon is with her daughters and Sly is studying who-knows-where, so I decide to take Ravi for a walk. My hometown isn't exactly interesting even if we took my car into town proper, so we agree on a simple walk amongst the color-changing leaves in my neighborhood.

After half-a-mile or so of houses, we come upon a clearing and a small creek with a park bench.

"And this is where I used to come to draw when I had to get out of the house."

"It's gorgeous," replies Ravi. We're both sitting on the bench as the cold air breezes across our faces. His arm is spread out behind me on the back of the bench. "Let me guess, you used to sketch that one rock over there." He points at one of the larger, jagged stones in the creek.

"How'd you know?" I ask him.

His arm manages to find its way to my shoulder pulling me in. "You like to zoom in on the little things, remember? You told me that the day you showed me how to find sight-lines."

"You remember all that about me?"

"Uh yeah." Ravi leans in closer. "We were in our own little bubble that day. Fuck, I wanted to kiss you when your head was near my shoulder."

I feel myself blush again as my eyes flick down to his lips. "Why didn't you?"

"'Cause I was scared shitless. And I didn't think you liked me." He's smiling and I lean into him, my lips a centimeter away.

171

"Well you should've. We could've been fucking way sooner." We both giggle as I lean in to catch his lips. Sparks fly as I slip my tongue into his mouth. I pull away reminding myself not to get too excited (why would I want to be hard out here in the open?), and I lean my head on his shoulder.

We stay that way cuddled up on the bench for a few more minutes, his left hand tracing little circles on my shoulder. Finally he breaks the silence by saying, "I have a really dumb question."

"Hit me, soccer captain."

"Co-captain." He clears his throat and I lean up to look him in the eye. "Have you taken any other guys here?"

"To this bench?"

"I know, it's dumb," he continues, looking down at his lap. "Everyone has a past. Except me, I guess." He shrugs.

"Yeah I suppose I went here with a boyfriend. Why?"

"Well I just..." He shrugs some more. "I don't like the idea of you having good memories here with someone else. Which is stupid 'cause you deserve your memories: your past, it's all yours, and, and-"

"Ravi," I firmly interject. "I only wanna spend time with you. You're my boyfriend now, remember."

He smiles. "I know. I just hope I can live up to the memories of these guys."

"One guy: Sean. And you've been here twelve hours and you're already leaps and bounds ahead of him. Got it?"

He smiles shyly. "I got it." I pull him into my shoulder and rub his back.

"Good." I kiss his head and we sit there in silence for a few minutes more.

--

* * *

Thanksgiving at the O'Rourke house is mildly chaotic. My aunts and uncles and cousins (girls, age eight and ten) arrive at around 1pm. We're all dressed nicely and there is plenty of delicious food, but having that many little ones under one roof is noisy at best. Since it's a decent day, Ravi and I help the girls play outside in the driveway. We grab some chalk and all four start doodling on the sidewalk.

At one point, Lottie and Lola run up to me and grab my hands. "Uncle Steven let's play hopscotch!" says one.

"Yeah I made a good one!" says the other.

"Mine is better!" says Lola (I think).

"Uhh..." I look at Ravi pleadingly. I am in no mood to hop up and down with five-year-olds.

"Hey, you know I'm an athlete," says Ravi, bending down to look at the girls. "I can probably do hopscotch better than your uncle!"

"Really? You're an athlete?" asks presumably Lottie.

"Oh yeah, he's captain of the soccer team!" I exclaim, able to wrangle my hands free. "Do you girls wanna show Ravi your hopscotch skills?"

"Yeah!" They both shout in unison, grabbing his hands and dragging him away. Ravi smiles his signature nervous smile at me one last time before being whisked onto the driveway. I beam back at him. He saved me, but he has no idea what he's in for.

I watch for fifteen minutes as Ravi hops up and down in his nice dinner clothes, doing whatever concoctions all four girls are able to create with chalk on the sidewalk. A strange sort of feeling floats through my chest as I see him playing with the kids. Sean never spent any holidays with us, and the girls were too little for him to play with when we were dating.

In this moment, though, seeing Ravi fitting in with my family? It does something to me. I can see glimpses of a future with kids of his own, and, just maybe, I'm sharing that future with him. It's like a warmth from inside me spreading outward. This handsome, sexy guy continues to put himself out there, all for my benefit and ask for so little in return. I refuse to say it out loud, even in my head, but it's so obvious what I'm feeling.

"It's lovely isn't it?"

"Huh?!" I squeak. I'm startled to see Sly suddenly next to me, drink in hand.

"The weather. What did you think I was referring to?" he asks with a smirk.

"Nothing," I lie. We stand there silently watching the girls laugh and play with Ravi.

"You should see your face, all dopey. It's hilarious," chuckles Sly.

"What?" I'm flustered at Sly's accusatory tone.

"I like Ravi. He's a cool guy. I can see why you're in love with him."

"Huh-what?!" I try to keep my tone even. "I'm not... huh?"

"I'm happy for you bro."

Before I can argue he walks away. Pretty soon, it's time for our Thanksgiving feast so we call all the kids inside.

As we enjoy the meal, Ravi sits at the kids table, listening to all their little stories and continues to entertain them. Eventually I join them, only half-listening as my thoughts dwell on my brother's words.

Ravi looks up at me at one point and smiles. He scoops up some pumpkin pie and feeds it to me on his spoon. We both giggle at nothing at all.

Sitting here at Thanksgiving with my family, my heart

thrums inside my chest as I finally admit it to myself: I've fallen in love. Ravi Metta has my heart, and I can only hope he doesn't drop it.

27: Ravi

Thanksgiving went great. Not to brag, but I really felt like I got along with Steven's family! I didn't feel any awkwardness, and I'd like to think I charmed them.

Saturday morning we pack up and leave, because as much as I enjoy sleeping in Steven's cramped twin bed, his roommate is still away, so we want to take full advantage of that. Private bedroom time is a rare commodity for us, so once we're back, we end up keeping as little clothes on as possible while we explore each other's bodies. We spend the entire day alternating between giving each other orgasms (anal, oral, handjobs- they all feel fantastic to me!) and cuddling. Everything I feel for him is so real, and inside or outside the bedroom, my hunger for him never goes away. I can only hope he feels the same.

With his roommate coming back late Saturday, I

reluctantly pry myself off of him. Going back to my dorm, I suddenly miss his warmth. I'd rather sleep in a cramped shoebox every night with Steven's heartbeat next to mine than in a king bed alone. I'm realizing the way I feel about him is crazy strong; it's dangerous, but I think I'm falling in love with him. What's worse is I don't want to stop.

--

It's a busy week as the semester is winding down. I don't have too many projects in art or my other classes, but Steven is hard at work matting his pieces so they're ready for his show. Once again, my soccer schedule gets in the way of us having a lot of time together, other than the occasional lunch date. My team is doing really well, winning game after game, but I'm so beat Friday night that I just pass out when I get back to my room.

Saturday morning the guys drag me to brunch. Landon insists we go because he claims we ought to enjoy ourselves because of the big semi-final game tomorrow ("It could be our last good meal together this season!"). I think he's being dramatic, but they're still my best friends, so I agree, after sending a simple *"Good morning gorgeous"* text to Steven.

As we get our food, I think about how much I miss Steven and I contemplate coming out to them. My whole livelihood in college is based on the team, but they're seemingly the last people to know I'm gay (except for a few possible outliers). I'm just too scared and don't want the dynamic to change. At the same time, the idea of Steven sitting front row at my games wearing one of my jerseys makes me feel all warm and tingly; it's a feeling I don't recognize, but I still want it.

I'm lost in my train of thought as I pay for my large bowl of oatmeal and side of eggs, when I spot my boyfriend in question sitting at a corner table, just like all those weeks ago. He's scrolling intently on his phone while sipping coffee. He looks adorable in his beanie cap and matching gray hoodie. Seeing him literally always makes me smile, and I beam even harder knowing that, unlike last time, he's all mine.

I consider sitting next to him when Landon walks up beside me and says, "Hey isn't that your art friend?"

"Huh?" I snap out of it.

"Come on," chimes Omar, striding past my other side. "Let's go sit with him!"

Oh boy. I did not expect this.

We approach Steven and he looks up at me, seeming pleasantly surprised. His smile, however, is short-lived as his face is now confused, seeing Landon, Omar, and Kareem, all sitting down next to him.

"Hey Ravi's art class friend. Steven, right?" asks Omar, plopping himself down right next to Steven. His shit-eating grin is not lost upon me as Steven replies by nodding and looking nervous. He keeps eyeing me for help, but I honestly don't know what to say.

"How was your Thanksgiving last week?" asks Landon, biting into a banana.

"It was good." His tone is wary, like he's being interrogated. "How was yours?"

"So boring," mumbles Landon with a full mouth.

The guys go back and forth (after I introduce Steven to Kareem) for a few minutes. They talk about soccer a lot, how annoyed they are at coach and some players, but otherwise the brunch small talk is harmless. Steven, though, is so quiet and reserved, it's like he's not even part of the conversation. He stops making eye contact with me all together, opting

178

instead to stare at his food. It brings a slight frown to my face, but no one seems to notice.

"Hey Steven," I chime in during the pause in the conversation. "Do you um, know when your semester art show is debuting yet? Is it next Friday or Saturday?"

"Oh yeah." He smiles at me, his eyes twinkling. "Prof. Garcia finalized the details and emailed me back. The big debut celebration is actually tomorrow evening."

"We have our big semi-final away game," remarks Omar while eating some eggs.

"Oh," replies Steven, looking down. His disappointed face physically hurts me. I want to go to his big debut so badly.

"But hey, I can come the next weekend, or after class sometime this week!" I hope my voice doesn't sound too apologetic.

"Yeah, it's open to the public for three weeks." He shrugs and his shoulders sag in defeat. I want to hold him so badly, but I can't.

"Speaking of celebrations, did you guys get your suits for the Athletics Formal?" asks Landon

"You know it," replies Kareem. "And my girl is gonna look fancy too."

"Lucky you already found a date," says Landon, disappointed. "Who are you taking Omar?"

"I don't know yet. I might go solo. I don't know if any girl can lock me down. Or guy for that matter."

"Please, like you'd ever bring a guy as a date to the Athletics Formal," scoffs Landon. "Two guys on a date, imagine?"

I look up and see Steven looking at me briefly before his eyes flick down to his food again.

"It's his ticket," states Kareem, looking down at his phone. "He can bring who he wants. We all get two."

"You all get tickets for your dates?" asks Steven, still not bothering to look up.

"Yup. Now I just gotta find a girl," replies Landon. "Speaking of, hey Ravi-" He turns to me. Aw shit. "Are we finally going to meet this mystery girl of yours?"

Shit. My eyes flick up to Omar's, whose eyes are blown wide. His eyes turn to Steven, and he's glaring down at his food, trying to burn a hole through the table.

"Uh well... um..."

"HEY KAREEM!" yelps Omar, causing us all to look up startled. "Um, are you going to um... STAY ON AS CO-CAPTAIN? For next year?" His voice is strained but he manages to steer the conversation away (for now).

"Yeah, why, you don't think I'm good enough?" Kareem replies, smirking back at Omar, challenging him.

"I don't know." Omar grins. "These freshmen are on the up-and-up, and they're coming for you."

"Fuck you," laughs Kareem.

"Excuse me, I gotta take this," Steven mutters, putting his phone to his ear and dashing away. The guys don't even say goodbye when he leaves, they're too busy arguing and laughing. I'd bet my laptop that no one was on that phone, that Steven was using it as an excuse to leave. Fuck. I know I hurt him. The guy I love more than anyone is hurting and it's all my fault.

—

Once I'm back in my room, I call Steven once every thirty minutes, only to go to voicemail. A few hours later, I finally catch him.

"Hello?"

"Hey Steven um…" I'm suddenly at a loss for words as I'm buttoning up my shirt. "Glad I caught you! About this afternoon."

"Look don't worry about it. Hey, are you free for dinner?"

"Ugh." I groan into my phone.

"Sorry I asked."

"No, it's not you," I reply, pulling up my pants. "Landon told me he wants to take me and Kareem out to dinner and talk about 'team strategy' or something. I don't know, but he's begging me. He says I haven't spent much time with him all semester, which, is technically true."

"I got ya," replies Steven. "I got the same shit from Dominic and Jenny."

"Right," I say, slipping on some shoes.

"I'm going to be putting up my work in the downtown gallery later. I'm so behind and the gallery opening is tomorrow. So I'm sorry we can't ya know… hang out or anything."

"I'm sorry too. About everything this morning."

"I told you forget it, it's not a big deal." I want to argue but then he continues, "Look I gotta go, um, but if I don't see you, break a leg at your game tomorrow."

"Same to you." With that, he hangs up the phone. I can't help but feel like nothing's been resolved, but soon enough, Landon is dragging me out the door.

--

We take the bus to Marino's, a nice Italian restaurant downtown. There's some mood lighting and plenty of tables with red-and-white checkered table cloths.

"Kareem is meeting us?" I ask, as we walk in.

"He was gonna bring his girlfriend, but he canceled, which is fine becaaaaause..." Landon drags out that word until we reach a table in the corner and I pause for a moment.

Sitting there are two girls, one of them the nude model from art class. What was her name- Brittany? Melanie?

"Ta DA!" sings Landon.

"Hey boys!" the girls say in unison.

I grab Landon and pull him away. "What the hell?" I whisper angrily.

"Look, I really wanted to take Tara to the Athletics Formal, but she'd only go if her best friend Bethany got to go. She needed a date, and so did you. So this is perfect!"

"Who said I needed a date?" I ask frantically, still trying to keep my voice down.

"It was so obvious that Omar was covering for you because you and your girlfriend broke up! So I hooked us up!"

"What? Wha... What?!"

"Look." Landon looks at me pleadingly. "I'm SO close to getting with Tara. Please just have dinner with us. If you don't wanna do anything with Bethany after the formal, then fine."

"I don't wanna do anything with her now!" My anxiety levels are rising.

"Dude, it's just a date. And you've been blowing me off all semester. When was the last time you came out and hung out with us, hm?"

I start to feel a little guilty and my eyes look down for a moment. "Please," pleads Landon. "Just two dates."

"One date," I growl, and turn back to the girls. Bethany is holding a chair open for me. As I sit down she sips some red wine and looks at me.

"Are we drinking wine already?" I ask, as apathetically as possible.

"Three glasses in, Ravi." Bethany winks at me. Across the table, Landon sips a glass while Tara giggles. This date is going to kill me.

28: Steven

I'm downtown at the Riverside Gallery, putting up the last of my works to showcase for tomorrow. It had been a long two hours of getting my side of the room ready for the big debut, and it had been an even longer semester. All of my best pieces were on display, and the entirety of my semester's grades would hinge on this showcase. The Riverside Gallery is made up of two large rooms, so with the four of us fine arts majors, we each got half a room to fill up. As I look around, a sense of pride swells in me; I'll never get over the feeling of displaying my own work for all to see. After a moment, my gaze falls on the orange-and-black of print of Ravi's toned body.

My thoughts find their way back to him. I had nearly forgotten the fiasco of this morning by doing all this work, and now I'm wondering where he is tonight. It was one thing to not want to come out to his team, but it's another to not tell me about this big formal for all the soccer players and their girlfriends. To top that off, he's not coming to my gallery opening tomorrow. I know I can't hold that against him, but it's all happening at once, and I'm starting to feel less and less like a boyfriend. I try to push that thought away with logic: Ravi cares for me and always makes me feel like I'm treasured. Yet, all of that goes away when he's around his team, which is a defining part of his life. I don't quite know where our relationship is headed, but I want everything with him so badly.

As I finish up to lock up the gallery, I hear a knock on the door. My heart leaps hoping that it's Ravi. Instead, I look through the glass door to see Sean walking in.

"Hey Steven." He smiles at me, but I stare at him, perplexed and annoyed.

"Hi." I don't even try to hide my irritation. "Look this is a private gallery, and I'm locking up."

"Wow, you've done some amazing work," he replies, ignoring me. Typical Sean.

"Thanks," I say, still annoyed. "Now I'm leaving so..."

"I really like your zoomed-in, found-object sketches."

"You never used to like them."

"Well they've grown on me." He turns to grin at me. I raise an eyebrow, my mouth still frowning. "Look, Steven, I'm glad I caught you. I've given it some thought, and... I miss us."

"Okay," I reply flatly. My heart is racing but I don't want to give him the satisfaction of my anger.

"You're amazing babe, and we were amazing together."

"You got bored of me. You left the country. And I'm not

your babe." It's taking all of my will to not just yell at him. Who the hell does he think he is?

"But we can be together again. I can make it work. I miss you." He tries to hug me but I instinctively pull away.

"Listen, I'm seeing someone else okay?" I'm livid right now. I open the door. "I don't think he'd appreciate what you're saying, and frankly, I'm not interested. So if you could please leave." I use my other hand to point out the door.

"You're not talking about that soccer player are you?" Oh fuck no. How dare he bring up Ravi? I'm so furious I can't even speak. Instead my jaw just clenches and I begin to almost shake.

"Look," he continues, almost smirking, taking joy in this conversation. "I get it, he's hot, but fooling around with a straight guy, the captain of the soccer team, is only gonna break your heart."

"You. Don't. Know him." I'm gritting my teeth and trembling in anger at this point.

"Babe, I didn't wanna say this, but... I spend some nights having wine at a bar at this restaurant two blocks away, Marino's. Tonight... in the corner booth, I saw your admittedly sexy boy toy on what looked like a double date. With a girl."

"Bullshit."

"Here, I took the liberty of taking a picture." He shoves his phone in my face, and lo and behold, in a dark corner booth, there's Ravi and Landon with two girls. No. No way.

"I'm sorry I had to be the one to tell you. Look, you and I can be an awesome couple again, babe. Just call me."

Sean walks past me out the door, but before he finally leaves, he turns and says, "Marino's is two blocks that way." He points down the street. "If you hurry, you can catch them if you still don't believe me. I'm sorry your straight boy toy went back to girls."

With that, Sean leaves, and I'm left simmering with anxiety while I lock up the gallery. He's a smug, narcissistic, manipulative asshole, but he did have photographic evidence. The time stamp on his phone was from twenty minutes ago and everything. The logical side of my brain tells me there must be some other explanation. Maybe it's his twin brother? Okay that's stupid, but I don't see how my boyfriend, the boy I've been falling in love with for weeks, could be on a date with a girl right now.

Fuck it, I need to know. I dash down two blocks to the bright red sign that says *"Marino's"*. As I contemplate walking in, I see the door open: out pops Ravi with a girl slung over his shoulder.

29: Ravi

I wish I could have drank during this dinner to make it more bearable. However, it was clear that someone here had to be sober. Why Landon was drinking so much the day before our semi-finals, I don't know. What I did know was that I had to drag Bethany's drunk ass back to her dorm.

As we walk out of the restaurant, I'm holding up half of her body as she stumbles. She did manage to mutter what dorm she was in, so at least I know where to tell the cab to take us. Before I can call one, I spot someone who stops me dead in my tracks and my throat goes dry instantly.

"Ravi?" Steven is standing right in front of me, and the tone of hurt in his voice is undeniable. His eyes are blown wide and are glossier than I've ever seen. I look down at Bethany, who's blissfully unaware of what's going on, smiling at me. She tries to kiss me for the nineteenth time tonight and I pull away (again). When I look back up I see Steven still standing in shock, trembling now. Shit.

"Steven, I can explain, ahh-" I have to push away Bethany's face again. That makes twenty times tonight.

At this point, Landon walks up behind me with Tara in tow and they're both tipsy and giggling. "Oh hey! Art guy!" says Landon.

Steven nods, still not taking his red eyes off of me. "Look," I sputter. "This isn't... I'm not..."

"We got ourselves hot soccer dates!" slurs Tara.

"Yeah you do," replies Landon, kissing her. "You're gonna be the hottest thing at the Athletics Formal."

"Hell yeah!" Tara and Bethany giggle in unison. Shit shit shit.

"Steven, it's not that... I'm not-" I try to plead, unable to finish a sentence.

"I hope you guys have fun at the formal," he says, his voice cracking, right before he dashes away into the night.

"No wait Steven!" I yell and plead. I want to cry, knowing I definitely hurt the guy I love.

"Jeez what was that fag's problem?" mutters Landon.

"Shut the FUCK UP!" I bark, losing my cool. "Don't you EVER CALL HIM THAT!"

At this, the three of them sober up abruptly, shocked at my outburst. I'm enraged and I don't even care who knows it.

"Sorry," says Landon sheepishly. I manage to pull out my phone in anger. I have one text from fifteen minutes ago.

Steven: "Hope your night is going well. I care about you a lot. You're the best guy I've ever known."

Fuck. I feel tears start to leak from my eyes as I swipe the message through so I can call a cab.

30: Steven

I turn off my phone as soon as I get back to my car. I drive to my dorm and find a pretty good parking spot. I get back to my room, take off my clothes, and dive into my bed

The next morning I turn on my phone to find a bunch of missed calls and text messages, all from Ravi. I don't read any of them. I slowly go to the dorm bathroom, take a leak, and take a shower. When I come back to my room, I curl up into my sheets again and go back to sleep. I know my wet hair will be a mess when I wake up, but I don't care.

Right now I don't care about anything.

31: Ravi

On the bus ride to the away game the next morning, I call and text Steven once approximately every five minutes. I don't like leaving voicemails, but the first text last night was explaining the situation, and each subsequent one today is a different version of "*I'm sorry. Please call me.*"

I feel my heart shattering in my chest. It has been over twelve hours since Steven walked in on my stupid drunken date that I didn't even want to be on. Now we have a huge game to play and my heart's not in it. This morning when I got on the bus, I immediately sat next to freshman Vince knowing that he wouldn't try to talk to me (after he greeted me, I just glared at him lifelessly and nodded). I'm glued to my phone the whole way, hoping, and praying Steven calls me back.

--

My prayers are answered in the away game locker room,

right before I put my phone away for the next two hours. My heart is racing as I leap up to answer it. I walk out into the hallway where no one's around and clear my throat before swiping the green "accept" button.

"Hello?"

"Hey Ravi." His voice is hoarse, but hearing Steven say my name feels like a glass of water on my lips, and I'm a man who's been drying up in a desert.

"Steven, I'm so glad you called! Did you get my texts?" My words are coming out quick and frantic, but I don't even care. He needs to know the truth.

"I did yeah..."

After a beat of silence I pry. "Um okay?"

"Okay," he replies, lifelessly.

"Look." I put my hand on my furrowed eyebrows. "I'm so sorry about last night. It wasn't even my idea, you have to believe me."

"I know Ravi. You wrote it all out." He sighs. "And I believe you."

"Okay?" Now it's my turn to wait for him to reply.

"Ravi, what are we doing?" He sounds so defeated and I feel myself panicking again.

"What do you mean?" My voice is starting to squeak. "I'm your boyfriend, and you're mine."

"I know. Ravi... I care about you more than anyone but last night... it was like all my fears became a reality."

"How can you say that? That meant nothing! It wasn't even a real date for me!"

"I know it wasn't a real date, but maybe it should have been."

"What?!"

"Ravi can you honestly tell me that one day soon you're

going to be able to take me out, hold my hand on campus, dance with me at a formal, give me flowers in public, or anything like that?"

"Huh, what? Steven I-"

"You can take that girl anywhere you want, and everyone will still adore you, but with me, we'll always have to hide half the time. It's…it's just easier with girls, isn't it?"

"I don't want any girls, I don't want anyone else, I want you!" I'm panicking, there's a pain in my chest, and I'm probably shouting, but I don't care. "Steven I love you!"

I hear him sigh over the phone, and after an eternity he replies, "I love you too, Ravi."

"Really?" I ask, grasping on to some ethereal hope. Please don't give up on us. Please.

"Yes… look maybe when you get back we can have a long talk in-person of where this is going."

"I'm not going anywhere," I say, barely a whisper.

He breathes out another long sigh. "Listen, I've got to go prepare for the gallery opening. I have to pick up a bunch of cheese platters and stuff… but um, hey good luck on the semi-finals!" He chuckles a hollow laugh. "Go KU Panthers!"

I chuckle back. "Thanks. Good luck to you too. Sorry I couldn't be there."

"It's fine," he says.

"Hey Steven?"

"Yeah?"

"I really do love you. And I'll never love any girl as much as I love you, please believe that."

"Okay. We'll talk tomorrow then." He sounds just as hollow as before, but I hold on to the hope that he believes that I love him.

--

I walk back into the locker room trying to hide the tears welling up in my eyes. I finish tying my shoes and it seems like no one notices my demeanor. It's not a big locker room by any means, and nearly everyone is done getting dressed. I turn off my phone and put it away (as per team protocol) and feel someone approach.

"Ravi, are you alright?" asks Landon.

"No," I mutter. Fuck no.

"What's wrong?" Of course Landon is probing, and this sets me off.

"Everything. Everything is wrong," I state, louder, my words starting to sting. I feel all my bottled up frustrations burst through. I stand up and raise my voice. "And I FUCKING blame you!"

I'm pointing my finger at his chest and he's looking at me in shock as he steps back. Everyone's officially stopped changing and listening to us, now and I don't even care.

"What?!" exclaims Landon.

"I didn't wanna go on a fucking double date yesterday, jeez Landon!" I'm shouting now, getting up in his space. Before either of us can get physical, Omar and Kareem get in the middle, Omar holding me back, while the rest of the team crowds around us. "And now I've fucked EVERYTHING UP!" Tears are starting to fall off my eyes when Coach Dacks finally walks in the room, getting in between us.

"What is going on here?" he demands. Everyone's staring at me now and all I can hear is my chest heaving and my heart beating. "Ravi?" Coach seems genuinely concerned while Omar still holds me back.

"What's going on?" I ask, incredulously. I look at Coach, then Landon, then Omar, then the rest of the team, all eyes on me. I take a deep breath. "What's going on is the guy I love probably hates me now because of that stupid date I was forced on yesterday! Yes, I have a boyfriend! Yes I'm probably gay or whatever! I hope that clears things up."

I'm taking in deep breaths while everyone in the locker room starts murmuring. "What?! What?!" asks Landon, in shock.

Coach shakes his head, his hand on his forehead. Great, now I'm done for. "Alright," he turns away from me. "Everyone out on the field to warm up. Landon, Ravi, come with me. You too Hall." He points to Kareem. "And you too I guess Odom." He points to Omar while he walks out the door.

--

We sit in the makeshift coach's office that visiting teams get at every school. It's only about two doors down from the locker room. There are two chairs other than the one for coach, so Landon and I sit while Omar and Kareem stand behind us. I wipe the tears from my eyes trying not to make eye contact with Landon while he stares at me. Omar closes the door while coach sits down and takes a deep breath looking down.

"Look," Coach Dacks begins. "I want to start by saying, you four are great players. Ravi, you and Kareem are great co-captains, and I know I made the right decision when I chose you last year. This season has been pretty good to us."

Well that was not what I expected.

"This semi-final game is a BIG deal. I… I need your heads in the game. The four of you are best friends, I see it on and off the field. We're starting in 15 minutes. I have like a hundred thoughts and strategies buzzing in my head, but all of that will go to the toilet if my players can't work out their shit before they walk out of the locker room."

I look up at Landon who's looking at me. We all nod.

"Ravi," he continues. "Is what you said true? Do you have a... boyfriend?"

"Yes," I reply. I pause for a moment. All of this seems so momentous. "I'm sorry but I can't... control who I am. If you don't want me on the team anymore-"

"Ravi, why would I not want you anymore?!" he exclaims, looking at me incredulously.

"Because..."

"You boys are in college, but you're adults. You're allowed to date whomever you want! I know you boys go out and drink and hook up or whatever. I was in college once too, you know?"

Landon and I exchange confused glances.

"But none of that ever affected your playing before, and I can't have it happening now."

"This was my fault coach," Landon says. I stare at him in shock. "I didn't realize any of this and... I dragged Ravi out on a double date and I think the guy he's with saw us." He turns to me. "I'm ...sorry. I didn't know." All I can do is nod in response.

Coach Dacks sighs. "Ravi, you're still a part of the team. I don't care about your orientation, but I DO care about the chemistry between my best players. That's you four." He points to us and we all exchange glances.

"Now Ravi, do you think you're going to be able to start in 10 minutes? I really don't want to have to bench you but with all the drama, I don't know if you have it in you to play."

"Yes I can," I reply quickly. I really want to, actually, to get my mind off of things.

"Good man, and if anyone on the team has any problem with gays or whatever..."

"I'll handle it," replies Kareem. I look up and smile at him. He looks at me grinning. "No one messes with the co-captains."

"Oh thank God," breathes out Coach Dacks, putting his hands on his head. "Now get out there please. You four are starting."

—

We end up winning and making it to the finals. It was a nail-biter for sure, but Kareem ends up scoring the goal that breaks the tie with an assist from Paul.

The game was so intense and the team is riding that sweet victory high that by the time I'm done showering, we've almost forgotten all the locker room drama from before. Of course, when I'm tying my shoes and turning on my phone, I suddenly remember it all: I came out to the team. Holy shit.

Still, Steven and I are up in the air, and it kills me not knowing about what's going to happen.

"Hey about before," says Landon, plopping down next to me. "I am... sorry."

"Oh, don't... don't worry about it," I reply, not even bothering to look up.

"Are we cool man?"

"Yeah, we're cool." I bump his fist, the universal sign of athletics forgiveness. "I just wish I could make up with Steven already."

"Isn't his art thing tonight?" Omar asks from the bench across from us.

"Yeah." I look up. "Too bad I couldn't go."

"The game got done pretty early," states Landon. I look up

to see hope in his eyes. "Maybe we can still make it?"

"We?" I ask.

"Grand romantic gesture!" squeals Omar. "I love it! Let's GO!" He sits down next to me shaking my shoulders.

I'm so confused. "You guys are cool with me... you know, dating a guy?"

"We don't care," says Kareem.

"Besides I already knew." Omar is smirking at all of us.

"What?!" exclaims Landon. "Who else knew?"

"I did." We all look up and see Paul holding up his hand.

"How the hell did the freshman know?!" Landon sounds mortified. I smile at his embarrassment.

"How did you NOT know? Ravi's always like staring at him, smiling." Omar laughs at me and I can't help but chuckle too.

"It's 'cause he doesn't share a wall with him in the suite," Kareem adds, laughing. "You guys are mad loud."

I feel myself blush, but it warms me up knowing my friends are still my friends.

"Not to interrupt," says Paul, as we all look up at him. "But if you're going to get to that art show in time, we should leave soon."

"Yeah well, the bus isn't ready, I bet," I reply.

"My dad drove me here." Paul shrugs. "I live near campus, but I can beg him to take us back like, now. He drives like a maniac on the highways."

"Yes!" shouts Omar, shaking me again. "Grand romantic gesture for the win!" We all laugh.

"You'd do that for me?"

"Of course. Come on, let's go." Paul smiles, waving us over.

"Ooh! Ooh! We need to make some pit stops on the way!" exclaims Omar.

"You're coming?" I ask.

"Dude, we're a team, right Landon?"

"Uh yeah," Landon nods, visibly confused. "What pit stops?"

"Have NONE of you watched a ROM-COM?!" asks Omar, incredulously.

We all stare at him in silence.

32: Steven

The turnout for my semester show is decent. There's friends, family, and fine arts faculty- no surprises here. Everyone's eating cheese crackers, drinking wine, and they all seem to be enjoying themselves. I'm standing in the corner near my side of the room where my work is on display. I've been here for two hours, as I'm mandated to stay for the whole debut. I wanted to stay curled up in my sheets in the dark, but now I'm dressed nicely downtown, trying to focus on the energy of the room. If I'm forced to be here, I might as well try to dwell on anything else to get my mind off of Ravi.

"They won their semifinals." I turn to see Simone approaching me. "It's on the school socials feed: real time updates and everything." I try to return my most genuine smile.

"Cool."

After a moment she continues, "Look Steven, you know Ravi is over the moon for you, right?"

"Mhmm," I mutter, not even bothering to look at her.

"That date was a fluke, it wasn't even real. I just think you should give him a chance. I've never seen you as happy when you're with anyone else or talk about anyone else."

"I'm talking about him right now and I can't say I'm thrilled," I remark, apathetically. Off in the distance, Prof. Irons talks to another faculty member. I'll focus on people-watching for now.

Simone stands next to me in silence for another two minutes sipping wine. Suddenly, she coughs, nearly spitting out her wine all over the floor.

I look at her confused. "Yes. Yes. Yes. Yes." She's chanting and nearly shaking, staring off outside the window. I look to where she's looking and my face goes pale; Ravi is stepping out of some car holding a huge bouquet of flowers. He walks into the gallery and looks around, presumably for me.

"Yes yes yes, things are happening!" squeals Simone. "Ravi!" She hollers and waves.

Ravi turns to look at me and, I know it's corny, but I swear, time stops. He looks damn good in jeans and a hoodie, and his eyes light up as he sees me.

I walk up to him, still probably pale in shock.

"Hey." He smiles at me.

"What are you doing here?!"

"I'm celebrating my boyfriend's gallery opening." He hands me the flowers. I feel butterflies in my stomach and every other romantic cliché.

"How.. what... huh?"

"I got a ride from one of the guys on the team. His dad drives really fast. I told him it was a 'love emergency'." He chuckles. "Do you like the flowers?"

I nod, my mouth still open in shock. All eyes are on us, but I can only see Ravi.

"I also have another surprise for you- more of a question actually." Just then, Omar, Landon, and another teammate of theirs walk in, holding large white poster boards. Ravi looks at them, nods, and they all smile back.

They flip over their posters to reveal big glittery words on them. Omar on my left has a sign that reads *"Will You Go,"* with Landon in the middle with a sign that reads, *"To the Athletics Formal,"* and the last guy's sign reads *"With Him?"*

What?

Huh? What?

"Soooo..." says Ravi, looking at me sheepishly. "I was hoping you'd be my date? To the formal?"

"You... they know?"

"Yeah, I kinda came out to them today in the locker room. Told them I'm in love with you. Which I am. So... will you?" He points to the signs. His teammates are beaming at me.

I have a thousand-and-one thoughts right now. Everyone's looking at us smiling. I want to reply so many different ways, say so many things. Instead, I drop the bouquet of flowers and grab Ravi's face and kiss him right then and there.

Everyone's applauding I think. People are clapping and hollering, maybe. I don't even know. All I feel is Ravi's lips on mine, and it feels like I'm home.

After we pull apart I see his million-dollar smile. "I take that as a yes?" I laugh and kiss him again.

--

Thirty minutes later, Ravi and I are cleaning up while I greet people goodbye.

"Best. Gallery opening. Ever!" squeals Simone as she hugs me and walks out the door.

"We've never had so many athletics people at one of our galleries before!" remarks Prof. Garcia as she bids me goodbye. Some time after Ravi's grand entrance, half the team came pouring in from a bus. Ravi said it was something about "solidarity"? They stuck around and were absolute gentlemen, mingling and eating all the crackers no one wanted to eat. No leftovers to clean up (score!).

Prof. Irons walks up to me. "Don't think either of you is getting an A just because of that romantic stunt." Ravi and I look at each other in concern. I turn back to see her smiling coyly. "You've both done great work this semester, so, you deserve high marks." We both breathe an audible sigh of relief. She leans in to hug me, and whispers, "I totally called it. I'm so happy for you two. Don't have sex in my studio though."

I'm sure I'm burning red by the time she walks out the door.

On our side of the gallery, it's just me and Ravi throwing away some trash in mostly silence. "Thanks for helping me clean up."

"What are boyfriends for?" He winks at me. I walk up to him and take his hand and kiss it against my lips.

"I still think we should talk, and now that the human garbage disposals on your team are gone, we can finally do that."

Ravi nods, nervously. "Okay."

"Ravi, I'm a mess. I lost my mind seeing you with a girl even though all signs pointed to it not being your fault. It was like all my fears came true. Sean told me you were leaving me for a girl and I immediately believed him and-"

"Wait what- Sean talked to you?!"

"Yeah, he was the one who saw you at the restaurant."

"What?! Fucking asshole!"

"I know he is, but that's not the point." I rub his hand to calm him down, and he places it against my cheek. "How can I be with you if all I have is baggage- the fear that you're gonna decide that being gay or being with me isn't worth it."

"Steven, you've made my life so much better ever since we've met. I came out and I get to be my most authentic self, and you're the reason why." He leans in and kisses me. It's soft and quick, but it means so much. "So whatever baggage you have, I'll take it with me too. I love you Steven, and I'm in this. It's you and me. Got it?"

"Got it," I reply leaning my forehead into his. "And I love you too."

"You know," he says pulling back, a shy smile on his lips. "Now that I'm out to the team..."

"Yeah..." I'm not sure where he's going with this.

"We don't need to sneak around anymore. You can stay over at my suite every night if you want."

"Really?" I ask excitedly.

"And I can think of a couple of ways to celebrate your gallery opening." He leans in to my ear and whispers, "Like using my mouth to make you come so hard you go blind." He bites my ear a little and I shiver.

"You know, this gallery is pretty clean now, we can probably go," I say in a rush, taking him by the hand and dragging him out the door while he laughs.

33: Ravi

We don't end up winning the finals the following weekend. We give it our best, and we're pretty evenly matched throughout the game, both sides blocking shot after shot. Unfortunately, their team manages to get a goal in during the last 15 minutes, and we don't come back from it.

After the initial sadness, Coach Dacks gives us a long speech on the bus ride home about how proud he was of us making it to the finals in the first place, something we hadn't even done the year prior. He is right though: we've come a long way, and we were playing better than we were last year. We just happened to be outmatched by a team slightly stronger than ours, and that's just the nature of the game.

In any case, Steven finds a way to console me that night, which honestly makes losing worth it (Steven O'Rourke can ride a dick when he wants to, I'm going to have to remember that!).

--

The week after, we're all walking into the athletics center, dressed to the nines. The events space floor is decked out in huge tables and lots of Christmas decorations- it was December after all, and the end of the semester was right around the corner. There's live music playing, and a huge designated dancefloor area; it's all gorgeous.

None of that compares to the guy wrapped around my arm as we walk in. Steven is in a white suit that hugs his thighs so perfectly. He's even lost the beanie and styled his hair back. He looks pristine, and I make a mental note to ruin his hairstyle later when we inevitably find our hands on each other tonight.

Seeing all the different athletics teams dressed nicely taking selfies near the Christmas decorations is a sight to behold. Coach Dacks is dressed well stancing with his wife, drinking something while chatting with Logan, who's decked out as well. No surprise Logan's here- this building is his baby after all.

I sit at the table and look around at my teammates: Kareem has his girlfriend, Landon is with Tara, Omar is solo ("*I told you, no relationships for this guy!*" he said), and even Paul brought a girl. We're all cracking jokes, eating food, having a good time- it's all perfect. With Steven's hand in mine and seeing all my friends, a sense of calmness washes over me.

This is it: the comfort I've never known. I had spent years feeling hollow when I wasn't actively playing soccer, like I could never be myself. I never thought an authentic relationship was in the cards for me, but along came this gorgeous artist who made stepping out of my comfort zone worth it. Now, with our friends supporting us, we've built a new comfort zone together, one that I want to share with Steven.

I see the live band (I think they're the music department?) and the empty dancefloor area and an idea forms. A surge of courage wells up within me and I look at Steven and smile. He smiles back, his hand in mine. "Come on," I whisper, standing up and pulling him with me.

"What?" he asks, confused, but stands up anyway.

I lead him to the dance floor. I hold up his right hand in my left and I put my right hand on his lower waist. His eyes shimmer and his cheeks redden, but when he finally puts his left hand on my shoulder, everything feels right in the world.

I see the live band discuss something, then they immediately shift to a soothing, slow dance melody. As we sway, Steven tells me, "This was pretty courageous of you, Mr. Metta."

"What? It's just dancing."

"Slow-dancing. With a guy. In front of all these athletes." I look over and see nearly everyone looking at us, muttering.

"I want them to know you're mine, Mr. O'Rourke." He chuckles and leans his head onto my shoulder.

"This might be my first time slow-dancing with someone I really care about."

"This is definitely my first time slow-dancing with someone I love."

He pulls away and looks me in the eye. He wants to ask me something, but holds back.

"Steven, you were my first a lot things, but I don't want any of this with anyone else but you." He smiles back brightly, and just like on the first day we met, I feel a warmth in me.

He leans in and kisses me gently. When I pull apart, I see Kareem and his girlfriend, Paul and his date, and plenty of other people slow-dancing near us.

"I hope not Ravi. 'Cause I love you, and I'm not going anywhere."

"I love you too, Steven." He puts his head on my shoulder and we continue to dance the night away.

Epilogue: Steven

"Do I look okay?" I ask, walking out of my room. "I've never been to like, a real dance recital before."

"You look gorgeous," replies Ravi, his eyes flaring with heat. I always feel self-conscious when he does that. He leans in and kisses me, his tongue sweeping at mine. A surge of blood rushes downward so I pull away.

"Okay, okay, we're gonna be late if we keep this up, hot stuff."

"I was waiting on you to get dressed, babe." We walk together out of my building.

Five months have passed since my big gallery opening. Ravi and I couldn't be happier. We spend a lot of time in his dorm because he doesn't have to deal with an actual roommate. His teammates keep complaining about thin walls, but I think they're just messing with him.

We're moving into an off-campus apartment together over

the summer so that solves any privacy problems. With us living together, next year is looking fantastic. Ravi's mom is slowly coming around to the idea that he's gay. He says that when they chat, she brings up all the successful gay and bisexual business men she's met over the years. While she may not be ready to join PFLAG yet, it's certainly a start.

When we visit my family, my parents are great with him and the twins, as usual, adore him (I think they both want to marry him!). Speaking of family, my brother is transferring to KU next year, so I'm looking forward to trying to get Sly to loosen up and have some fun.

The soccer team re-elected Kareem and Ravi as co-captains again for our senior year, with the approval of Coach Dacks. The spring season doesn't have nearly as many practices or important games, so we've had more free time this past semester.

When we're together, everything feels fantastic. We hang out with his friends and my group as well. We openly hold hands and go to restaurants when we can. At night, we discover all sorts of different sexual ways to excite each other. I also may have done some nude modeling for Ravi myself, giving him a new-found appreciation for the sketchpad I got him for Christmas. I guess he has an art kink now?

Speaking of arts, tonight we're walking into the fine arts building, hand-in-hand. "I thought you knew this place?" asks Ravi.

"I've never actually gone to the large performance space! I'm a visual artist, not a dancer."

"Hey, I didn't know Landon was a dancer either, but here

we are."

"We're gonna be supportive," I reply as we file in line. "Just like we were supportive of Logan and his recital."

"Yeah I know, I mess with Landon a lot because he's a loud-mouth, but I think this dance thing he's doing is pretty cool. I bet it's the reason he's mellowed out so much this semester."

"I don't think it's the CLASS so much as a certain-" Ravi bumps my shoulder to get me to stop talking, and we both laugh.

"Look," I continue. "All I'm saying is that he discovered something to love in the arts, just like you did." I smile at him brightly and he smiles back, leaning to kiss me.

"I'm lucky I was forced to take that class. I never would've discovered the sexiest guy ever." He rests his forehead against mine.

"I'm the lucky one." I pull away and look at him. "Seriously, what did I do to deserve you?"

"Hey, you gave me the courage to come out and be myself. On top of that, you're amazing, talented, and gorgeous. Face the facts Steven- I scored up when I got with you!"

I giggle and kiss him. My heart feels just as warm as the first time we kissed, and I still haven't gotten over it. "You're not so bad yourself, soccer captain. Thanks Ravi... for loving me."

"I'll love you as long as you want me around." He winks. I lace my fingers into his and walk into the performance hall, knowing that I don't see myself ever letting this man go.

(The End)

Thank You

Dear Reader,

Thank you so much for going on this journey with me! This was very much a labor of love, and I hope you enjoyed Ravi and Steven's story. My goal is to reach as many people as possible with this novel and shed some warmth and comfort in these trying times.

It would mean the world to authors like me if you gave this a review on any book-review website. See the next page for links to my socials.

Stay tuned for more, the "Artists and Athletes" series is just getting started. I think you know whose story might be unfolding next, so keep an eye out for my upcoming releases to watch the continuing adventures of your favorite soccer boys discovering a new found appreciation for the arts.

Never stop loving life and never stop reading,
  CD Rachels

About the Author

About the Author

CD Rachels has been coming up with stories since he was little. At first it was all about superheroes and pocket monsters, but his genre of choice has expanded since puberty.

He's been consuming young adult gay fiction since he was a teen, but within the past five years, he's moved up to the big leagues of gay adult romance. In 2020 during quarantine, he burned through more male/male romance books than he ever had in the previous 29 years combined.

He lives in New York City with the love of his life and works in health insurance. When he's not reading and writing, he's playing board games and practicing music. He is honored to become a published author, and if you're reading this, your support means so much to him that it's giving him a tingly feeling (in a good way).

Follow him on Instagram: https://www.instagram.com/

cdrachels/

Or join his Facebook group "CD Rachels' Chill Discourse Room": https://www.facebook.com/groups/ 1356048148159801

Made in United States
North Haven, CT
26 January 2022

15331027R00124